Checkmating the Duke

Cassie O'Brien

Chapter One

My cousin, Bonnie's, sweet voice accompanied the warm breeze wafting through the open window I'd set ajar to refresh the unseasonal, torpid October air in my bedroom.

"Run, run, my little lordship. For when I catch thee, I am going to tickle you until you squeal."

George's high-pitched laugh gave tell as to his age. "No, naughty Bon-bon. You shall not. For I am faster…"

I smiled and returned my attention to my body servant, Hannah. She reached into my clothes press and presented me with a gown. I nodded my assent. She folded it and placed it into my travelling trunk while I listened with pleasure to the sound of feet scrunching on the gravel path below my open casement and my child's breathless giggles, until the beat of not-so-distant hooves sounded and his merriment ceased.

"Bon-bon, be that Great Uncle John astride the chestnut?"

"That it is, Georgie. Let us away before the riders come closer."

I stiffened at the thought of such an unwelcome visitor and nodded at Hannah. "We will resume our efforts later."

She bobbed her curtsey. "As it suits thee. I could attend to the packing of your petticoats and stockings in your absence, my lady?"

I nodded, left the room, and skittered down the stairs at a pace fast enough to ensure I reached the Great Hall before my guest.

Bonnie burst through its door a couple of minutes after me, a frown marring the smoothness of her fifteen-year-old brow. "I have returned George to Goodwife Alice's care in the nursery. What on God's good earth is Uncle John doing here? It can be for nothing wholesome, I am sure."

A spurred footfall echoed on the flagstones in the entrance hall "You should have remained with George, child."

Bonnie's face flushed to the stamp of her foot. "I turn sixteen next month. I am no longer a child and will not be treated as such."

I looked at the rich sheen of the newly purchased blue satin gown she should not have been wearing until her name day and glanced my warning at her. "Then kindly cease to act like one and do not to alert our uncle to that fact. Make yourself scarce before he catches sight of you and decides to interfere in your business as he does mine."

Bonnie's expression froze as the awareness of her danger dawned, although the rest of her moved. She picked up her skirts, dashed away, and concealed herself behind a tall carved side screen.

I dipped my curtsey to the correct depth required to acknowledge the exulted rank of my guest when he strode through the door then gave him my greeting. "Your Grace, welcome, although you catch us unprepared. My apology. Refreshment suitable to combat your long ride

3

would have awaited if I had but known we were to be honoured by your presence here this day."

He walked closer, his thin frame no longer clad in the puritan severity his dour heart favoured, but in a coat and breeches of russet brown—a suit more in keeping with the mode of the moment, although still plainly finished and unadorned by such fashionable furbelows as ribbons or lace. He huffed testily and stripped off his riding gauntlets. "Bah! Unexpected, after you were so unaccommodating to your father's request? A tankard of porter will suffice, if you have it?"

A demand, even if disguised as a question. I looked over his shoulder at the reddened face of my elderly steward, Willikin, patently exhibiting all the signs of one who had struggled to keep pace with an impatient guest.

"Yes, my lady," he wheezed. "It shall be immediately to hand."

I inclined my head with a smile to signal my forgiveness at his failure to perform his duty and announce my visitor prior to them descending upon me without due notice. "As soon as may be managed, if you please."

He bowed. "At once, my lady."

Willikin shut the door behind him.

I noted the glower in Uncle John's eyes and sought to steal the wind from his sails by sinking down onto a chair and inviting him to do likewise. "An arduous journey, Your Grace. Will you sit a while and recover your ease?"

He slapped his gloves across the palm of his hand with an impatient grunt, but good manners held, and he did not remain standing when requested to do otherwise by a seated lady. I acknowledged the courtesy with a graceful nod as he sat in the chair opposite mine then guided the conversation towards that of more normal courtly etiquette.

"My aunt, your duchess, you left her well and in good health, I hope?"

His brow cleared at the mention of the one thing he loved as much as he did the accumulation of wealth, although I knew better than to think the subject I was sure had brought him to my door, would be long out of mention.

"A little gout has arrived for her with this warm weather, but 'tis no worse than her usual affliction, and all things considered, she remains in fine spirits. We visit Tunbridge, so she may benefit from drinking the waters next week."

The door opened. Willikin walked in, a serving tray in his hand and, standing on it, a pewter tankard, a snifter of brandy, and a stemmed, fluted glass. "A raspberry cordial, my lady?"

5

I nodded towards the occasional table beside my chair. "Very agreeable, I thank you."

He set down my glass and offered the tray to Uncle John. "Your Grace. Porter to refresh your thirst and something to aid your recovery from the exertion of your ride?"

Uncle John grunted his assent. "Very well. Put it down then take yourself off. I require no further interruption while I converse with my niece."

Willikin did so then bowed himself from the room.

I sipped, appreciating the refreshing tartness of the unsweetened concentrate of berries while Uncle John drained his tankard then picked up his brandy.

"So, you wonder at my arrival here while I wonder at you turning down your father's offer of succour in your time of grief."

I twitched the dull, grey material of my skirt to draw his attention to the colour of it. "I appreciate his efforts, but as you see from my half-mourning, I've had six months to become accustomed to my new circumstances."

My uncle opened his mouth to speak.

I cut him off before he could do so. "Let us speak openly. You and my father wed me at fifteen to a man old enough to be my grandfather for the generous grant of land Earl Summerly would settle on you should I provide him with the heir his late wife could not. My lord husband was never uncivil towards me, but I will make no pretence to feeling a distress deeper than I would for the passing of an intimate acquaintance."

Uncle John swallowed a mouthful of his spirit. "Well said, Emma. You were ever a sensible girl who knew what was due to the family, as we now only seek to lift the burden from your shoulders. Sign the management of the Summerly Estate over to those of superior intellect experienced in such matters, then you may return to pursuits more suited to your feminine nature such as the mothering of your son."

I sipped a little more cordial while I pretended to consider the matter, then gave him a slight shake of my head. "I do not believe that will be necessary, Uncle. My husband may have been considerably older than me, but he was not in his dotage. He knew he was likely to predecease me and appointed a good and trusted man to manage the estate on George's behalf should the need arise. Indeed, the revenues have risen under Mr Fitzwilliam's care."

He tossed down the remainder of his brandy. "Bah! This estate should be consolidated along with others owned by the family until George comes of age. Free yourself from the burden of overseeing the income of it, and I will guarantee another lucrative marriage for you."

My skin goose-bumped at the thought of the allowable excuses he would invent to divert the revenue of the estate away from George's future funds and into his own coffers, and even more so at the prospect of another joyless union with a bridegroom of his choosing. "Sir, I must beg your indulgence to be given more time before I contemplate such a step. My marriage may not have been a love match, but my husband is barely cold in his grave. It would not be seemly."

My uncle nodded towards my pimpled arms. "I can see the thought disturbs you as yet. I praise your good heart in honouring Earl Summerly's passing so will not press the matter at present...though plums such as Viscount Edgeware do not come along ripe for the plucking very often."

I tried to summon a face to match the name but failed with only one fact coming to mind—the viscount's father was the Duke of Wight, a close contemporary of my uncle, and as such, it was just as like his son would be cut from the same miserable cloth as they were. "My apology, I do not recall Edgeware."

Uncle John shrugged. "No, you wouldn't. He's been out of the country these last three years. Took it into his head to go a-voyaging hoping to discover new lands. He failed and came home three months ago with his tail between his legs, but still, he's the only heir. Poor old Wight only produced a basketful of girls apart from him."

Feeling I'd dodged a well-aimed arrow, I inclined my head and stood, obliging him to follow suit. "I thank you for your consideration in visiting me today and for your understanding of my need to take a little time to sort my jumbled thoughts, Your Grace."

He set his brandy glass down on the table and sniffed. "Yes, well, don't take too long about it. As I said, the prize of an heir to a dukedom will not be on the marriage market for long."

He stood and picked up his riding gauntlets. "Although now I come to think on it… How old is that young cousin I left in your charge after her parents' unfortunate demise?"

I stiffened then relaxed my shoulders and tried for an appearance of nonchalance with an airy flick of my hand. "I can't say I've given the matter of her age much thought, Uncle. Miss Bonnitta currently resides in the children's quarters with

George. Will you take any further refreshment before you leave us?"

Uncle John pulled on his gloves. "Shame. Mayhap she would have done just as well as you had she attained sufficient years to have begun her womanly flow, and no, I thank you. The brandy was an overindulgence I should not have accepted. I will not compromise my well-being by digesting anything more before my supper. I shall allow you a further month of mourning for you to settle your nerves, but when I return, madam, it will with the expectation of your sensible decision regarding the management of this estate and also towards Edgeware."

I inclined my head. "As you will, Your Grace. I wish you safe travels, and please pass my felicitations on to my aunt."

He nodded and strode to the door.

I closed it after he walked into the hallway and hissed. "Stay where you are. Don't you dare come out until we are sure he has gone."

We held still until the jingle of reins and hoofbeats sounded beyond the window.

Bonnie moved from behind the screen. "Cousin, you are such a fibber, and I thank you for it. Who is this Edgeware? Is he as crusty as Uncle John?"

I wrinkled my nose. "If our uncle stands on such terms with him as to be confident he will take one or other of us to wife, I would assume so."

Bonnie sat in his recently vacated chair. "What will you do when he returns next month?"

"Not be at home. I'll extend the length of my stay in London from what I originally planned but I'll admit to being concerned we have come to his notice just now. Our uncle is a duke, the head of our family, and what he determines holds sway over we single females whether we be widowed or unmarried. I have fobbed him off for the present, but by whatever means, it is more vital than ever that during my visit to London, I attract the king's notice so as to be able to plead our cause."

Bonnie giggled with the overconfidence of inexperienced youth. "But how could you not? Your hair is pale and luxurious and your features praised by every male who sets eyes on you."

I shrugged. "What is considered beauty in the small pond we inhabit may well fade to ordinary when set amidst the glittering array of females displaying their charms in the capital. King Charles is infatuated with his fiery-haired mistress. He insisted on her appointment as a

Woman of the Bedchamber even in the face of his new bride's objections. That Barbara Palmer has bewitched the king and holds him in her thrall, even to the discomfort of his queen, is well-known."

The smile left Bonnie's face. "But your request will not be onerous on him. You only require a few minutes of his attention to set out our case, and surely with your godmother agreeing to present you at Court that will be achieved?"

I squared my shoulders. "We must hope so, for all our sakes, but I begin to believe it will be as well for you and George to remove to Hatfield while I am from home. I would not put it past our uncle to invent an excuse to take George into his custody and reinstate his guardianship of you if he returns here and discovers I am not."

A tear sparkled in Bonnie's eye. "I would refuse to go with him. I will hide and I will hide George with me until he goes away again."

I shook my head with a smile at her mutinous expression. "Yes, I daresay you would, but as brave an action as that would be, as solitary females, our best chance of defence comes from thinking ahead of him and thereby thwarting his plans. The manor I hold for George at Hatfield is small but comfortable and a mere twelve miles from London. Return to your room, and I will send Hannah to pack for you."

She stood and offered her hands to me. "I never cease to be glad it was your household Uncle John placed me in when Mother and Father died."

I took them with a soft squeeze. "Nor me, for you are the younger sister I never had. Now run along, but speak of this to no one but Hannah. The time for the remainder of the household to realise you are leaving will be when you, George, and Goodwife Alice take your places inside the coach two minutes before my own departure."

Bonnie kissed her fingers at me and trotted from the room.

Willikin, who like any long-serving retainer must have been hovering outside it awaiting fresh instruction, entered less than a minute later and stated the obvious. "My lady. The Duke of Portchester has left the house."

I inclined my head, and the mantel clock chimed noon. "His Grace did not require any midday refreshment. Before mine is served, I would like to speak with Goodwife Alice in the library, and also Mr Fitzwilliam if he is within and has not ridden out."

Willikin bowed. "Indeed, he is here and preparing for quarter-end in the estate office. I will summon them immediately." He rounded up the empty glasses, set them on his tray, and followed me from the room.

I turned right. He swung left and clicked his fingers to attract the attention of the young page sitting on the chair in the entrance vestibule. I walked into the library, sat behind the desk, pulled a vellum sheet from the drawer, and dipped my nib into the stand dish.

Willikin opened the door as I laid the quill down. "Goodwife Alice and Mr Fitzwilliam as requested, my lady."

I dismissed him with a nod and acknowledged their presence with another after a bow and a bobbed curtsey. "Alice, I believe George requires a change of scene during my absence. Have him and yourself packed for an extended stay as to be ready to accompany me on the morrow and alert no one else you will be doing so."

Alice nodded. "As it pleases thee, my lady."

I gave her leave to depart the room, and when the door closed behind her, looked at Mr Fitzwilliam. "Take a chair, sir?"

He sat before the desk, his black hair fashionably long but tied back to suit the efficiency of the tasks he undertook riding all over the county on my behalf and fixed his clear green-eyed gaze on my face. "Something troubles you, my lady?"

Three years my senior and the second son of a well-to-do land-rich baron for whom the usual occupation of a commission in the army had not found favour, he had worked alongside his father on his elder brother's behalf with diligence but little prospect of reward until my late husband had recognised his qualities. An offer of suitable renumeration along with the prospect of preferment in his own right enticed him to us two years gone, and in the six months of my widowhood I had come to value his advice, and even more, his lifting what burdens he could from my shoulders onto his own rather broader ones.

I sanded the vellum and offered it to him. "My warrant passing the welfare of the Summerly Estate to you, and you alone, while I am away?"

Understanding gleamed in his eyes as he took it from me. "An honour, my lady. You and your son's interests will be safe in my care. Where will you take him?"

I smiled at my lack of need to explain my newfound desire for George not to remain at home without me following the visit from my uncle. "Them. His Grace has emoted the idea of Viscount Edgeware as a soon-to-be future bridegroom for either myself or Miss Bonnitta. My standing as a widowed countess will allow me to withstand his urgings should it become necessary, but he is Bonnie's legal guardian, and I'd lief not see her married before she knows aught of the world."

"As you were?"

I nodded. "Yes, as I was. My lord husband was as considerate to me as was in his nature to be, but I would not willingly see Bonnie go from nursery floor to marriage bed as I did. Without notice, they will step into the coach with me tomorrow, and I shall install them at Hatfield on my way to the capital."

He smiled. "The final staging post before London you've not frequented in years that has passed out of most people's remembrance?"

I returned his smile. "Yes, and should my uncle arrive here with a verbal instruction from me in my absence, it will not be genuine. If a missive comes bearing my name, likewise, unless it contains the word 'trust' or more particularly, I *trust* my message finds you well and *entrust* you to undertake…"

His nodded. "Be reassured. I will not mistake the matter. Nothing will occur here you should not wish for before you return."

My breath caught at the sincere warmth in his eyes along with an urge to be on the other side of the desk held in his strong arms while he soothed away my fears. I swallowed, recalled my wayward thoughts, and ended our conversation by offering him the back of my hand. "You are kind, sir, and I thank you for your consideration in caring for the estate according to George's best interests while we are from home."

He lifted it to his mouth, and my heart beat harder at the feel of his whispered kiss.

"As ever, I am yours to command. Safe travels until we meet again."

I watched his tall, upright figure leave the room and lost myself in the imagining of his lips on mine, then other places besides until the mantel clock chiming the half-hour brought me from my reverie. I shook the pictures from my head, blushing at my body's longing response to them, then left the library to go in search of my midday meal.

Chapter Two

The following morning, I consigned my grey gown to the duster bag, donned my new mulberry carriage dress, and completed my toilette by way of a wide-brimmed hat embellished with a fashionably jaunty yellow feather. The additional luggage was stacked amongst mine, and I took my place in the coach as it was loaded. Hannah climbed in and sat opposite me. Silas Coachman stepped up onto the box, his whip in hand to control the team of four impatient horses when the remainder of our travelling party marched outside and boarded before the groom could shut the coach door.

I knocked on the roof to give Silas the signal to move off. The groom slammed the door, and George laughed as the team cantered down the drive, the horn sounding its warning to the gatekeeper to open them.

"Mama... Alice says this is a secret adventure."

I held out my arms, and he jumped onto my lap.

"But Bon-bon says we are going to a haunted house and may see ghosts."

I shook my head over his shoulder to Bonnie's shrugged smirk then ruffled his blond curls. "Should you do so, call Alice. She will dispatch it with a good thump from the poker beside the fire. Now look through the window and tell me how many cows you see."

We pulled up at Bedford coaching inn after two hours of George's counting—"One, two, three, four and a pig inna pen...five, six anna chicken coop."

The ostler caught the lead horse's head, and another released the steaming team from their traces. Serving girls brought hot pies and tankards of beer to the coach on trays and offered them in exchange for the return of a coin. I lowered the window, passed over two silver sixpences, and received their blessings for purchasing the lot.

"The Lord love yea, my lady. Thankee…"

We took a pie apiece and refreshed our dry mouths with the beer then threw the tankards out of the window for the serving girls to recover as Silas whipped up the fresh team. An hour later, we cantered past Hatfield House, the abode of a young Elizabeth I at which she had received confirmation she had been made Queen of England, then through the village of Hatfield itself and onto a four-square manor house that sat to one side of the road that led away from it.

Silas halted the coach, the footman opened the door, and Mrs Goodenough, the housekeeper, rushed from the house clutching her apron.

"Oh, my gracious! 'Tis my lady! We have looked for you these last three years gone and wondered if we would see thee again, yet here you are with the young heir if I'm not mistaken."

I alighted from the coach and beckoned George to follow me. "'Tis indeed. My son and cousin require respite from the bustle of daily life, so I have bought them here to enjoy a little peace and quiet while I attend my godmother in Town."

Bonnie exited the coach after George, followed by Alice to my introduction.

"My cousin, Miss Bonnitta DeVere, the Earl Summerly, and Goodwife Alice, his dry nurse. I am due to arrive at the Duchess of Melville's residence today so must be on my way."

The footman unloaded their trunks to the change of horses, and George wrapped his arms around my knees.

"I will miss you, Mama. Must you go?"

I bent and kissed into his soft blond curls. "Be brave, my little man. Bon-bon is here to care for you."

George let me go in preference to concentrating on a late-season bumble bee buzzing in the flowerbed beside him, and I held out my arms to her and kissed her cheek.

"Less than twelve miles," I said. "Just over an hour at full gallop. Send for me if anything occurs to disturb you. Sign the message with George's familiar name for you to tell me it's truly from you."

She lifted her chin and squared her shoulders. "I will take good care of George, I promise."

I took her hands and squeezed. "Of that, I'm sure. I will write to you of my progress, but sign my note with a single capital 'E' so you may know the truth of the news you receive."

"Oh, please do, cousin. The thought of being here without knowing what is occurring with you discomforts me the most. With that assurance, I can be more at ease."

I smiled, remounted the coach, gave Silas the order to move off, and the footman blew the horn to signal our arrival when we drew up at the portico of my godmother's London mansion an hour and a half later. Liveried servants appeared out of its grand entrance to bow me in.

The Duchess of Melville, older and plumper than I remembered her, held out her hands as my name was announced in her drawing room. "Come, come. I've been expecting you this last hour or more."

I moved into her embrace and kissed her rouged cheek. "My apology, Godmama. A small detour was necessitated by His Grace, my uncle. I'll explain when we are alone."

She brushed her lips along my jawline towards my ear and murmured, "The damned man's a menace. I'll await your telling of it. Now, come and renew your acquaintance with Francombe. He runs with a younger set that will better suit your years than mine own friends and has announced himself honoured to squire you around Town during your visit, though he cannot quite recall you, for you have been buried in the country for such an age."

I smiled, and she led me to her son, known by one of his father's secondary titles until such time as he inherited the dukedom.

Slim, tawny-haired, and a vision to behold, wearing a long-skirted coat of peach satin embroidered with gold thread over cream silk knee breeches, he lifted my hand to his lips and gazed into my eyes. "Welcome, most beautiful lady. Are you dreadfully fatigued from your travels? Your radiance suggests not."

The duchess laughed. "Desist, Franny. Emma has spent most of the day on the road to reach us. Save your flummery and court manners for when she has recovered from her exertion."

The sparkle of good nature flickered in his lively blue eyes, so I answered in kind. "Fatigued, sir? How could that be with the sight of your divine loveliness to refresh me?"

Godmama tapped his wrist with her fan. "I can tell the two of you are destined to get along famously, but run along now, Franny, so Emma and I may partake of a dish of tea."

He huffed a theatrical sigh. "To be dismissed so soon. How will I bear it?" Then he planted dainty kisses across each of my knuckles. "Until later, my delectable one. If you are not in danger of collapsing from your efforts today, I will see you at dinner this evening?"

I suppressed a giggle at his outlandish performance, took back my hand, and placed it over my left breast. "Be still my beating heart. My dear sir, until we meet again, I bid you a fond adieu."

He snorted a laugh. "Mama, I declare you have deceived me. Fresh from the country, you said. The lady will shine at Court. I know it."

I dipped him a curtsey at the compliment. "Mayhap with you as my muse, my lord."

He bent his knee, rolled his arm, and gave me an extravagant three-fold bow. Two lackeys sprang to attention and opened a door each for his exit.

The duchess clicked her fingers, and a maid swooped in bearing two dishes of tea aloft on a silver tray. I followed my godmother towards two cushioned chairs set each side of a pedestalled table. We took our places, and the maid set our hot drinks before us. I removed my hat as she dismissed the servants with a wave of her hand, and she waited for them to withdraw before she spoke.

"I believe from the manner of your replies you know better than to take Franny's compliments to heart?"

I sipped the refreshing liquid from my shallow dish. "We are not so far from London at Summerly that word of the current mood in the capital escapes us. Indeed, gossip of the licentious freedom currently enjoyed at Court wings its way to me each passing day with the absence of the one who previously discouraged the delivery of booklets and broadsheets."

She sipped from her own dish. "My condolences on his loss, but freed from the taint of your husband's puritan leanings by his passing, with a hale son to secure the wealth of the estate to you, most would consider your current position enviable. Yet, the tone of your letter to me suggests this is not the case?"

I set my tea-dish down on the table and offered her the explanation she sought. "Uncle John and my husband trod a fine line between the Roundhead and Royalist causes, managing to offend neither and thereby retaining their wealth—but Cromwell's Protectorate was ever their preference. My husband's influence over me is no more, and I would escape my uncle's if I can. He is an avaricious man. I believe his beady eye is fixed on me, hoping to find reason or excuse to declare himself custodian of the Summerly Estate in my place. I will resist him but would lief not spend the years of George's minority looking over my shoulder awaiting his next move. Then there is Bonnie, of whom I am very fond. I will not see her fall to his machinations if aught I can do prevents it."

She nodded. "And your father? Where is he in all of this?"

I shrugged. "As he has always been. Subservient to the more forceful personality of his eldest brother."

She tapped her fingers on the table while she considered the matter. "You have not left your son at home without adequate protection?"

I shook my head. "No. I have taken him and Bonnie to a safe house in my absence. The estate I have left in the care of a man I trust. He is the younger son of Baron Fitzwilliam and committed to Summerly for the chance of betterment my late husband offered him. A good man. Loyal and true."

She smiled. "A rare creature indeed, then. Guard him well. Now tell me of Bonnie, who I presume is Miss Bonnitta DeVere, the only offspring of your father's first cousin, Harold?"

I nodded. "A sweet girl Uncle John placed in my household when she was orphaned at eleven. She has little wealth to back her, other than she bears a noble name which His Grace will use when the opportunity arises for him to bartor it in exchange for a few shekels into his own purse."

"And your plan to prevent all you have described to me from happening…?"

"To attain a private audience with King Charles and petition him to name George and Bonnie as under his protection so future decisions of import concerning them will be scrutinised, if not by the king himself, at least by an impartial judge."

She narrowed her eyes and surveyed me appraisingly. "The king is a notable connoisseur of female beauty, and you have enough in form and face to attract his attention, but that alone may not give him pause to grant your request unless you are intending to allow him to bed you?"

A ripple ran through my belly, as it did whenever I contemplated the carnal reputation of our Sovereign and the thought he may wish to do more with my body than lift the hem of my nightgown and thrust his shaft inside me for three minutes of his own grunted pleasure before leaving my bed to return to his own. "I believe I am. According to a certain pamphlet that has come my way, King Charles wields a mighty cock, and the squeals of delight emanating from his mistress ring around Whitehall nightly, which will at least be an improvement on what has been my lot up until now."

Her laugh pealed out. "Rochester's rhyme reached you in the country?"

I quoted a stanza. "'*Nor are his high desires above his strength: His scepter and his prick are of a length.*'" Then joined my laugh to hers. "It most certainly did!"

She intoned another. "'*Tis sure the sauciest prick that e'er did swive. The proudest, peremptorious prick alive.*' Oh, how I wish I were still young enough to discover the truth of that! I can see you are going to do well at Court, Emma. Your maid should have unpacked for you by now. Let us go and inspect your gowns. Your carriage dress is handsome but not quite the latest style, and you must be dressed to perfection, à la mode, if you are to achieve the impact you desire and turn the king's eyes away from Mistress Palmer in favour of his spending the evening in your arms instead."

She stood and led me upstairs to my guest room, although when she opened the door, I realised it was a suite with a sitting room, bedroom, dressing room, and a small personal closet for my commode. I looked through the open, connecting doors at opulent soft furnishings of peacock blue embroidered with birds of paradise in silver thread and thanked her.

"These rooms are beautiful. I did not expect such an honour."

She looked around the room. "I believe there is enough floor space for the gallants that will crowd in here when you undertake a Grande Toilette."

My pamphlets having let me down on that particular subject, although not wishing in any way to appear a green girl, I had no choice but to ask, "Ah…my Grande Toilette? When would you suggest?"

Her bright-eyed gaze still darting here and there, she answered with noticing my hesitation. "Not more often than once a week. That Barbara Palmer draws a crowd each morning is understandable, but no other beauty could match that interest. I would advise you to make yours stand out for being rarer than hers. She rises around mid-morning, so call yours for an earlier hour."

I ventured a tentative question in the hope of garnering more information on what would be expected of me. "Nine of the clock, or maybe ten?"

She tapped her foot and gazed into the far distance while she thought. I listened carefully to the mutters emanating from under her breath.

"Maid wakes you. Necessary private time. Dress hair. Don fresh smock and return to bed. Admit admirers, yawn prettily while you pretend to wake up and they proclaim their wonder at you doing so. Step into your petticoat and gown to their appreciative compliments. Add the time needed for stockings, garters, and shoes." She sighed, refocused her eyes. "It will have to be no later than nine of the clock, I fear, or your swains may well depart to attend of Mistress Palmer's toilette before you have permitted your favoured one to tie your garters and slip your shoes onto your feet."

I bit my lip to prevent my grin as I pictured the scenario while she continued.

"Still, Franny will escort you to her Grande Toilette if you wish to take note on how your rival conducts herself during them. Now, let us inspect your choice of gowns."

I bit down harder at the thought of him doing so. "I will consult with him at supper this evening."

She smiled, and I led the way towards Hannah hovering, twitchingly nervous. I nodded my encouragement at her. "Lay my new gowns on the bed for Her Grace to view, if you would?"

She bobbed and did so.

My godmother examined and plucked at them then delivered her verdict. "Fashionable enough, but the necklines are too modest. You are not some virgin bride in need of a husband but a beautiful, young widowed countess with a child. Lower the bodice to show the rise of your breasts to just above the blush of your nipples and remove enough material to display more of your neck and shoulders." She turned to Hannah. "I expect your mistress to be suitably attired in one of these gowns in good time to sit to her dinner this evening?"

Hannah curtsied. "As it please thee, Your Grace. I am quick and neat with my needle."

"As I would hope. The rose-pink in the first instance, I think."

Hannah lifted the gown and went in search of her work basket.

Godmama kissed my cheek. "Now, rest a while so you do not fall asleep over your dinner, and I will see you later. We congregate in the Tapestry room at seven of an evening. Call for a servant to show you down until you find your way around."

I kissed her back. "I thank you for receiving me in your home. For this beautiful apartment and your kindness to me."

She pinched my chin. "I loved your mama and miss her. I will deny her daughter nothing that is in my power to grant."

I smiled, and she left me, then Hannah released me from my travelling dress, stockings, and shoes, and I lay down on my bed in my under-smock and did as I had been advised.

Chapter Three

Hannah woke me at five. I yawned, stretched, then walked to my dressing room. A steaming pitcher of water stood on the washstand. She poured into a porcelain bowl, added a splash of distilled rose essence and a small jug of white wine, then unbuttoned and removed my day-smock. Naked, I held my arms out to each side for her ministrations. She dipped a sea-sponge into the scented water and, squeezing and refreshing it with every stroke, wiped my body from neck to feet, then patted my skin dry with soft cloths and dusted it with lavender-scented talcum powder.

Refreshed, I thanked her and lowered my arms for her to place an evening chemise over my head, then stepped into a ruffled white satin petticoat she fastened around my waist. I raised my arms again. She lifted my gown over my head, fluffed it over my petticoat, raised the side of it, and pinned the folds she gathered at the level of my hip to show the underskirt, then added a knot of ribbons. She added more ribbons to adorn the short, slashed sleeves, and I was ready to receive my stockings, garters, and shoes.

I surveyed the result in a Chevelle looking glass. Hannah's alterations had changed a beautiful but modest evening gown into one of sensual frivolousness, the sight of which would have my late husband turning in his grave. I turned away from the mirror with a satisfied smile and entered my bedroom to see the fire burning brightly, having been made up in my absence, and a very welcome goblet of ruby-red wine standing on the consul table.

Excitement bubbled in my belly in anticipation of the adventure about to begin after years of a drab, colourless existence, and I sipped some wine to calm my nerves. Hannah offered me my jewel chest, the contents of which had been locked away for the entirety of my marriage.

I decided. "The diamond clips for my hair, I think. The pearl earrings, bracelet, and my grandmother's ruby ring."

She retrieved the items and set them down beside my ivory stick fan. I sat and sipped while she refreshed my ringlets with the curling irons she heated in the fire, after which she applied a little blacking to darken the fairness of my lashes and brows, then brushed a touch cochineal across my lips to deepen the blush of them. The mantel clock chimed seven as she gathered my curls and clipped them away from my face with the sparkling diamond bars while leaving a few ringlets loose to frame each side of it.

I picked up my fan and stood. "Call for a footman, if you would."

She opened the door and hollered my request. "Man required to attend Countess Summerly in her rooms."

I squeezed her hand to acknowledge my appreciation of her skill in dressing me—she had originally been in my mother's service.

Hannah's eyes crinkled at the corners. "Your appearance is beautiful, my lady, and your Lady Mother would have rejoiced to see it so. Grey, black, and white were never her colours of choice."

I gave her a quick, impetuous hug. "Your day has been longer than my own. Do not sit up in the chair and await my return. Rest on the chaise longue in the sitting room, for I may be out until the early hours."

She curtsied her gratitude. "I thank thee for thy consideration, my lady. I shall seek a little supper at the servant's table then willingly stretch out upon the day bed so as to be refreshed to attend you on your arrival home."

I smiled and followed the lackey from the room.

He led me down two flights of stairs then along a hallway to the double doors at its far end, flung them open, and announced in ringing tones, "My lords, ladies, and gentlemen. Lady Emma Bonneville, Countess of Summerly."

Unfamiliar faces turned towards me, and I hesitated until Franny stepped forward and offered me his hand.

"Beautiful lady, I see you have recovered from your journey in time to join us. I am overcome with joy to see the vision of your loveliness."

I swept him a curtsey, took in his suit of yellow brocade threaded through with gold, and put my hand in his. "I would have travelled twice as far to gaze on the sight of you clad thus, my Adonis."

He tucked my arm through his and led me forward, speaking softly. "Dryden was stood to the side of you. I swear I heard the scratching of his quill noting our exchange for a future production."

I spoke equally quietly, feeling at ease in his company as if we'd conversed daily for years. "I will look forward to our caricatures' appearance on stage in due course."

"His latest production opens in Drury Lane tomorrow afternoon. Shall we attend?"

"That would be delightful. Your mama suggested I hold a Grand Toilette and attend Mistress Palmer's in your company to learn the way to go on if, indeed, it is acceptable for me to do so?"

He smiled. "Of a certainty, it is. A female attired as a male is all part of the fun."

I choked down a giggle at the thought. "I do not possess male clothing."

"Then we shall make our way to the vendors of the Royal Exchange in the morning to outfit you."

Lord Francombe put faces to names for me as we moved through the room, and dinner passed in a noisy whirl with conversation flowing freely up and down the table until it was time for the guests to disperse—most to join my godmother at her card tables to play Basset or Loo, although two rather elderly couples called for their carriages to return home in search of their beds.

Franny stood at my side, and we nodded, bowed, or curtsied our farewells when the room emptied, then he offered me a soft cloth-of-gold mask.

"If you are not fatigued, we could attend a masquerade being held at Rochester House tonight?"

Excitement tingled through me at the prospect of an evening that did not end with the completion of dinner. I accepted the mask with a wide smile and secured the ties at the back of my head, so it covered my face from my forehead to the bridge of my nose. Franny donned his own, guided me to the Melville carriage, and butterflies tickled my middle when the high-stepping pair moved off.

"Which of the Wits shall I see?"

His eyes glinted behind his mask. "Of the Merry Bunch, Buckingham and Berkeley should be at Rochester's side. Of the others, I would expect Hobbes and Sheppard to be present along with the Duke of York."

I could not keep the glee from my voice. "And Bennett? Killigrew?"

He laughed and pinched my chin. "Have you been so very starved of company, lovely lady?"

I smiled and nodded my affirmation. "Yes. Also of laughter and the pleasure of another's conversation for its own sake."

He raised my hand and kissed the back of it. "Then your enjoyment of tonight's entertainment is assured. I can vouch there will be an abundance of both. The Peerage, actresses, whores, fops, and men of genial nature will mingle freely without any formality due to condescension of rank."

Anticipation shivered down my spine to my delighted smile. "Wonderful!"

The carriage halted at a mansion built of cream-coloured stone blocks, lit by two score or more of flaming flambeaux whose dancing yellow light shone bright enough to illuminate the whiter wattle and daub of the humbler half-timbered houses surrounding it. A footman opened the coach door. Franny stepped down then assisted my descent. I laid my hand on his offered forearm, and he escorted me in. The buzz of chatter along with the sound of unrestrained laughter greeted my ears when we entered the ballroom, and within a few short paces we were surrounded.

"Francombe, who is this angel? Present me, I beg?"

"Divine creature, I would worship at thy feet…"

"Beautiful lady, my lips beseech to kiss your hand…"

"Her name, Francombe? I demand it!"

Franny dismissed their enquiries with a dramatic wave of his hand. "I shall not say. Begone, you rogues. We are masked and incognito. This angel's name is mine, and mine alone tonight. You shall know it when the time is right for you to do so."

A fair-haired beau, with a head of blond curls that fell past his shoulders like mine, cut into the side of us, gazed into Franny's eyes, and traced his finger over his lips in a gesture so intimate I smiled as understanding dawned.

"A rival for me, Franny? Are you sure?"

Franny bit down, and the beau snatched his finger away. "Mayhap a blonde angel, warm and loving, is preferable to one formed of ice." He put his arm around my waist and pulled me close to him.

I turned my face into his shoulder to hide my giggles. "Lord Francombe, I declare! Have you only invited me here to incite another's jealousy?"

He waited for my laughter to subside then spoke into my ear. "No, not just for that. Your riposte to my sallies when we first met this afternoon inclined me to love you from the start. We are not destined to be lovers but friends, tight as ticks. What think you?"

I kissed his neck under his ear to facilitate my soft reply. "My blood relatives are formal and cold. If you would be brother to me, I will be sister to you, though the rest of the world need not know it till we decide they should."

He stepped back and swept me an extravagant bow. "My angel, you are everything I hoped for and more. Shall we dance?"

I curtsied my acceptance, laid my hand on his, and he led me to the center of the ballroom to join the Gilliard, the steps of which I knew courtesy of a passing dance-master whose services I had engaged for a day. We dipped, smiled, twirled, and moved between partners along the line until we met again at a four-handed reel. He pressed my hand, and we exited the dance.

"Come, sweet one. My desire to drink from your shoe overcomes me. Slake my thirst, I beg?"

43

My laugh near snorted down my nostrils. I took his hand and muttered sideways, "And once you wet my shoe, I am expected to place my foot back in it?"

"Alack, the sacrifices we must make in the pursuit of true love and devotion…"

I let go of my laugh to join those of many others echoing around the room. "Outrageous, Franny! If you ruin the satin of them, you shall buy me a new pair on the morrow."

He captured a glass from the tray of a passing lackey. "Of course, my rosebud. As many pairs as you like so long as I can taste the nectar of your pretty little toes tonight?"

I flicked open my fan and used it to cover my somewhat less-than-flirtatious, wide-mouthed grin but raised my skirt and displayed my ankles to cries of wonderment from half a dozen gallants who gathered around us when I did so, and Franny knelt. He removed my shoe, poured, drank, then replaced my sodden footwear.

I fluttered my fan and peeked at him over the top of it. "My dear sir, how you adore me. I will return the favour in a suitably wet moment as soon as I am able." My swains gaped at my double entendre, and I swatted Franny's arm with my fan as we walked away. "By pushing you into the nearest midden should you be close by me on the next occasion I come across one."

He laughed and led me back to the dance which soon turned into a romp when the pace of the music picked up to the tune of *Cuckolds All Awry*.

By four in the morning, the ballroom started to empty.

Franny tucked my arm through his and signalled a lackey to call for our carriage. "Let us away, exquisite one."

His blond-haired beau, lounging to one side of the door to our exit, stared at us, then more particularly and obviously at the roundness of my breasts rising above the lowered neckline of my gown, a faint smile playing in the corners of his lips. We drew level, and he moved his gaze to Franny's face, ran the tip of his tongue over his top lip, then kissed two fingers in his direction.

I held my peace until our carriage pulled away then asked as I removed my mask, "A silent message to you?"

Franny untied his own and shrugged. "He is a keen connoisseur of variety in his bed and indicates his pleasure would be excited by both of us joining him there."

I smiled. "With my apologies, that particular activity will not be taking place."

He kissed the back of my hand. "Alas, no. It will not. The thought may alight his senses, but joining my apologies to yours and to all females for my lack of prowess, the sight of your Lady Garden would leave my Little Dickie nothing but unresponsive."

I giggled.

He grinned then added, "But enough of that. Let us indulge ourselves in a scintilla of speculation as to the Duke of York's absence from tonight's festivities and leave Edgeware go hang."

I could not keep the note of surprise from my voice when I compared the reality of the man with how I'd imagined him. "Edgeware! That was Edgeware?"

"His name has meaning to you?"

I shrugged. "Not as such. My uncle brought his name to my attention recently, so in my mind's eye I presumed Edgeware would be another such as he—a dry old stick."

Franny smiled. "No, capricious and arrogant when the mood takes him, but never that. How came His Grace to mention him?"

"He's being touted around the marriage market by his erstwhile sire."

He laughed. "Oh, that's ripe! You are the mysterious heiress Edgeware is being prompted to make up to?"

I huffed. "Well, if I am, he had best go find another. The percentage of income from the estate my late husband willed to me as my portion I consider mine to spend, but the remainder will be staying where it belongs, held in trust for George's future funds. On that I am determined."

He frowned. "The disposal of the annual income of the Summerly Estate is within your remit?"

I nodded. "The underlying wealth and assets are secured to George, but the yearly revenue is managed between myself and my late husband's equerry, Hugo Fitzwilliam."

Franny blew a soft whistle through pursed lips. "I cannot see that as less than forty thousand gold crowns. A tempting prize, indeed."

I admitted the true figure. "It has become nearer fifty under Mr Fitzwilliam's management, less his salary and entitlement to a quarter share of any increase in the estate's income going forward year on year."

He squeezed my hand. "A mere drop in the ocean compared to the whole. Dearest heart, you are going to be pursued from pillar to post by those seeking to capture that amount of funds."

I thought of my father's visit to me at Summerly, then my uncle's. "The chase has already begun. 'Tis why I am here. To gain the ear of the king and seek his protection."

"So, your visit to us is not merely for pleasure? You have a scheme in mind to secure your independence?"

I nodded. "Yes. For myself, George, and also that of my young cousin, Bonnie, who resides in my household. Your mama knows the detail of it, and I have her support."

"Will you not share your plan with me also?"

I hesitated. "If Edgeware is part of the chasing pack, I'd leif not make you privy to a confidence that requires you to choose between myself and a more intimate friend, now I know his identity."

Franny smiled. "Do not hold back, dearest one, for the attraction you sense is in no way a meeting of hearts and minds to demand Edgeware and I share our secrets with one another."

I squeezed his hand, then admitted, "If I can persuade King Charles to take an interest in George's and Bonnie's welfare and commit his intent to do so on paper, I will be able to spoil the plans of those who would seek to meddle in our lives for their own advantage, though your mama advises I must bed him to fix his attention on the matter in hand."

He laughed his appreciation of my plan. "Oh, very good. That will halt the hounds baying at your heels, for sure."

I smiled. "So, to entice him away from Barbara Palmer for an evening, you would advise?"

He considered the matter for a few moments, then suggested, "That we continue our little charade of this evening until your official Presentation at court. You will appear in His Majesty's eyeline—beautiful, mysterious, and unnamed. Our campaign will begin at the theatre tomorrow—my box is beside his own. Dress in a gown more suited to a ball than an afternoon entertainment, and as it is not untoward for a lady at the theatre to be masked, wear that also."

The carriage drew up at our journey's end, and I hugged him to me as our route to our bedrooms led in differing ways at the top of the stairs. "I thank you for taking my part in this."

He pinched my cheek. "We shall triumph, my sweet, with pleasure to be enjoyed for both of us in the game to be played along the way. Let us reconvene in the drawing room at eleven of the clock in the morn in readiness for our trip to the Royal Exchange?"

I smiled my acceptance then left him, entered my guest suite, and found Hannah, fresh-faced from her rest, making herself at home by rearranging the order of the dresses in my closet to her satisfaction—"Silver first, then the blue…" She looked up and exclaimed when I shut the door with a yawn as my day of travel coupled with my staying up until the early hours caught me.

"My lady, you are fatigued, and no surprise with dawn near broken."

I walked farther into the room. "I am but I have had the most wonderful time. I must sleep now, but wake me so I may be dressed in my mulberry gown ready to accompany Lord Francombe on a shopping expedition at eleven, if you would?"

She bobbed her curtsey in acknowledgement of my request then removed my clothes down to my chemise, and I snuggled under the coverlet. Hannah carried them to the dressing room to attend to any repair or cleansing needed from my wearing of them.

I woke to the tinkle of china. Hannah walked into my bedroom holding a mahogany tray. I sat straighter for her to set down the food and drink to break my fast across my lap and breathed in a heady aroma of spice. Soft, warm cinnamon rolls were sitting on a plate beside a bowl of hot cocoa, and I broke pieces from them, dipped them in the creamy, mocha mixture, and relished each delicious mouthful.

Hannah left the room while I ate and returned carrying a jug of steaming water as I swallowed the last delectable morsel. I swung my legs out of bed, followed her to the dressing room, and gave her advance notice of my intention to bathe later in the week.

"I would like to immerse myself fully, including my hair, on the day of my presentation to His Majesty."

She nodded and poured hot water into my porcelain wash bowl. "I will order a tub to thy room and require the footmen to fill it, my lady."

Excitement quivered through my belly. "I wish to appear at my best, clean of body with my hair freshly dressed and, I think, with the sparkle of diamonds to bear complement to the sheen of my silver gown."

She dipped my sponge into the scented water with a soft, fond smile. "You will shine with a brilliance to hurt the eyes, my lady. I promise."

I returned her smile and lifted my arms for her to cleanse my skin, then she dressed me in my mulberry gown and feathered hat. The mantel clock struck eleven, and she handed me a satin wrist-pouch containing my gold crowns and silver coins. I tripped down the stairs to meet Franny no more than fifteen minutes after the appointed time and found him sitting in the library, reading a pamphlet he laid down when I entered the room.

"My congratulations, dearest heart. I had not even finished reading the cover page."

I walked nearer to admire the emerald-green brocade of his coat, and he rose to his feet.

"The sight of you delights mine eyes, as ever, my Adonis—and I am not a slug-a-bed, you know."

He smiled and offered me his arm. "I am in awe, my love, but do not look for the same from my mama. You will find her in no public room until at least two hours after noon."

I laid my hand on his forearm, and he led me outside to the coach. We stepped into it, alighted outside the Royal Exchange, and made our way to the gentleman's outfitters that enjoyed his patronage. He made my requirements known, and in less than an hour I had purchased a pair of white satin knee breeches that moulded themselves to my form tightly enough to obtain his approval, a fine lawn shirt, a ruffled satin-and-lace jabot that tied at the neck, and an embroidered brocade waistcoat of such tight fit, that although I dressed as a male, the outline of my breasts showed clearly I was no such thing.

I blushed at the sight of my lower body on such obvious display as I viewed my completed outfit in the mirror, and Franny grinned.

"Excellent! We shall attend Mistress Palmer's toilette tomorrow. Leave your curls undressed to fall over your shoulders, but for now let us return home so you may attire yourself *a la femme fatale* for the theatre."

I smiled, took his arm, and he led me back to the coach.

"And you, Franny? What colour will you wear? I have several ball gowns I could choose but would prefer to complement your appearance rather than we clash."

He thought for a moment then said, "Blue. I have not worn my suit of it these last three days. Do you possess a dress of lemon or gold?"

I sighed with satisfaction at the opportunity to wear it. "I have a gown of cloth of gold with an under-petticoat of peach silk."

His kissed his fingers at me as the coach pulled up. "Superb! The performance begins at two but is always behind time. I shall await you in the downstairs hall at a quarter past the hour so we may arrive before curtain up but fashionably late and cause a stir at our entrance."

I puckered my kiss back at him then ran upstairs to Hannah. Sitting in a chair, her workbasket alongside it, she was altering my green dress. She tried to free herself from the flounces of material of it, and I waved her down.

"Finish your seam but tell me please if you have completed your work on my gold gown?"

"Yes, my lady. I amended the silver first, then the gold, before starting work on this one."

I smiled. "I would wear it to the theatre this afternoon, if you please?"

She laid her work aside and stood. "Your good spirits brighten my heart, but first some food? An orange or two eaten during the performance will not be enough, I fear."

I turned my back to her. "Very well. I will take some bread and cheese with a glass of port, but redress me in my gold gown, and I will inspect the jewels in my box while you fetch it."

She did so, and while she was gone, I selected a circlet of filigreed gold set with opals for my hair along with pearl rings and matching bracelets to accompany it, then nibbled on my repast. When she returned, she rearranged my hair and refreshed my face with a smudge more blacking and cochineal. My mask was where I had laid it, on the nightstand beside my bed. I picked it up, fastened the ties, then glanced into the mirror.

Hannah looked at my reflection and handed me my fan. "Your mama would have been delighted to see you thus."

I picked up my skirts and acknowledged her good wishes with a quick smile over my shoulder as I left the room.

Franny waited at the bottom of the stairs, and his eyes lit up at the sight of me. "I swoon before thine beauty, most gorgeous angel. We shall flirt so prettily, it will be swords at dawn between the outraged admirers you will gather, I am sure."

I swept him my most graceful Court curtsey in practice for when I would have to perform it in front of the king. "My Lord Francombe, 'tis my pleasure and honour to attend this performance with you."

He took my hand and assisted me to rise. "Come, dearest one. Let us set the cat amongst the pigeons by the lateness of our arrival."

Franny handed me into the coach and said when it set off, "Mistress Palmer has recently received a gift of state apartments close by the king's own at Whitehall, so we shall make our way to them on the morrow by way of the water."

I didn't hide my surprise. "She has? The queen has given way to his mistress being raised to a status equal of her own?"

He shrugged. "'Tis the fate of a princess of no particular beauty when she is accepted in marriage on the promise of a large dowry, of which her mother only pays half, and that in the form of sugar and spices rather than the gold coinage as was expected. Still, the king is kind to her. He did not repudiate the proxy marriage as was his entitlement when the truth became known and pays his attentions to her nightly in the hope she will, at least, provide him with a legitimate heir."

I glanced at him. "I thought he spent his nights with his mistress?"

He laughed. "My dear love, King Charles' cock is a veritable man o' war—a canon that never ceases fire. He spent the night before his wedding in the Palmer's arms—and she is rumoured to be as insatiable as he, then wedded his bride, and after the ceremony, attended to his mistress' needs again before satisfying his new wife."

I giggled. "Good Lord!"

Our carriage halted in front of the theatre, and street hawkers bearing trays of sweetmeats crowded around it, but fresh from the country though I was, I knew better than to encourage them by any sign of interest and stared straight ahead. Franny reached into his pocket and threw an array of small copper coins high into the air. The urchins screeched and dispersed in search of them, leaving our path clear.

Fawning ushers, in hope of their own share of coinage, bowed our way to Franny's box then bustled about us, repositioning chairs to improve our view of the stage and offering their services to bring us any refreshment we desired. Franny winked at me his satisfaction at their noise then guided me towards a seat. I sat and added to the fuss by busily rustling my skirts to arrange them to my satisfaction.

He dismissed the ushers with a silver sixpence a piece then sat beside me, his blue eyes alight with amusement, and murmured, "The king's box is to our left."

I twitched open my fan, glanced over his shoulder, and saw our entrance had the desired effect—King Charles, a head and shoulders taller than any other in his box, was looking our way. I met his eyes, and a small smile played across his mouth as he acknowledged my presence with a tip of his head. My tummy fluttered at the sensuous fullness of his lips, and I pulled my gaze away to my blushing thought of their soft plumpness on my naked flesh and surveyed my surroundings instead. Our boxes were decorated with the same green baize that covered the seats of the semi-circular tiers of benches in the Pit below me. Above it, a great glazed dome allowed the ingress of daylight to supplement the glow of candles, which even with mirrors placed behind them to magnify their output, could not, on their own, illuminate the stage.

Franny leaned closer. "Your blush becomes you. He has smiled in your direction?"

I nodded, and he squeezed my hand.

"When the stagehands begin to clamber up the ropes, there will be an interlude for a scene change. The occupants of the boxes move freely between them during the breaks, so to avoid any enquiry as to your name, I suggest we disappear from here and view the second half from the Pit where the glory of your gold dress will cause quite a disturbance."

I looked at the broiling mass below us of those who had crowded into the theatre to watch the production, not having the wherewithal to pay for a box. Orange sellers moved amongst them, crying their wares with some being hoisted to shoulder level amid much good-natured banter to launch their produce upwards into the waiting hands of those who called to them from the boxes, then just as deftly plucking a coin from the air as payment was returned to them.

"Oh, yes, if we may?"

The opening lines of the drama rang out, so he nodded his silent reply, and we focused our attention on the stage where I promptly lost myself in the wonder of the story taking place before my eyes until Franny nudged my arm to draw my attention to several small figures climbing upwards at the side of the stage. I put my hand in his, and with barely a rustle from my dress, we slipped through the door of the box and made our way downwards.

He smiled. "Beautifully done. Let us take our time and allow a few minutes to elapse before our reappearance."

We slowed our steps, and when we finally reached the outer edges of the Pit, my gold gown worked its magic—the whispering, pointing crowd parted before us until we achieved our aim and reached the center of the Pit. The sight of a silver half-crown in Franny's fingers caused two young men, so alike as to be brothers, to jump to their feet and state their happiness to watch the remainder of the play standing at the back. Franny thanked them for their consideration, slipped the nearer of them the coin while he did so, and they departed with the means to pay for a dozen further performances should they wish to attend them, although I thought the more likely outcome would be of the coin heading in the direction of the local ale house as soon as the play ended.

We sat. Franny purchased an orange, peeled it, and offered a segment to my mouth. I parted my lips to accept it, looked upwards, and saw King Charles standing at the front of his box gazing in our direction. I ate my slice with a murmur of pleasure at the taste of its tangy juices on my tongue.

Franny asked. "'Tis sweet?"

I nodded, and he fed me the rest, piece by piece, to various nudges and winks from those sitting around us at the slow, teasing show he made of doing so. The cast returned to the stage as I swallowed the last mouthful, and I fixed my eyes upon it and joined in with the enthusiastic applause when the actors took their final bows.

Franny stood and offered me his arm. I laid my hand on it, and the crowd parted before us once again. He led me from the theatre, assisted me into the coach, and I sighed.

"I thank you. The performance was wonderful. All I hoped for and more."

The horses set off, and he smiled. "Then my happiness is complete, although, my sweet, I must desert you on our return home. I am promised to attend Prince James' bachelor party tonight to play dice and Deep Bassett."

I untied my mask. "May good fortune favour you in your games of chance, and I am more than happy to give homage where 'tis due and attend your mama here this evening at her card tables of lower stakes."

Chapter Four

F ranny and I parted ways at the bottom of the stairs with a promise to meet again at ten of the clock in the morning to attend Mistress Palmer's toilette, then I made my way to the Tapestry room to join my godmother and her guests for dinner. She sat me between the Lords Exeter and Saltash, and I ate a very pleasant meal in their company talking of the various entertainments on offer in the capital while they vied with each other to place the choicest morsels of every remove onto my plate.

We walked to the card room afterwards, and my godmother nodded at the table next to her own to signal me the honour of hosting the game of Loo.

I smiled with an assurance I did not feel, never having played the game excepting those hands I had dealt to myself in the library in practice for my visit, then sat in the chair with stacks of coloured counters before it and picked up a pack of playing cards. I started to shuffle them, praying they would not slip through my nervous fingers and spill upon the floor. The table filled, and I looked at the faces ranged in front of me, happy to see Exeter and Saltash had elected to play with me.

"So, my lords and ladies, your preference for the stake is…?"

There were five calls of "sixpence as usual" to three of "a shillin'", so I pushed a shallow dish forward.

"Sixpence a counter it is then. At thirty counters to the stack, two gold crowns, and one half-silver assures the play."

Coins were dropped into the dish, and I began to deal the pack around.

"First knave begins the game…"

Play continued until my godmother emitted a small yawn as the clock struck two, and her guests, noticing the signal, played their last hands. A delighted Lord Exeter, having won four dishes of coins, kissed the back of my hand then the pulse of my wrist.

"A pleasure to have been in your company this evening, my lady. I bid you a fond goodnight with my hope I will see you here again?"

I inclined my head. "My visit to the duchess is of several weeks' duration, so I will join my hope to yours and presume you will."

My godmother held her arms out to me when the room emptied. "Well done, Emma. You were a resounding success. Was it also so at the theatre?"

I walked into her embrace and kissed her cheek. "Resounding? I am not quite so sure, but King Charles noticed my person, so that I will count as a measure of success."

She squeezed my hand. "Of course he did. Now away to bed with you. Black shadows under the eyes are not becoming."

I smiled at a gentle admonishment that spoke of her caring for me in the way I did Bonnie. "With my thanks for your looking after me, goodnight."

She patted my arm, and I left her, walked to my bedroom, and Hannah's gentle snores emanated from behind the sitting room door which she had left set ajar. The plump pillows awaiting me looked so inviting I slipped off my shoes and stockings, removed my own dress, and blew out the candles. My eyelids fluttered closed as I snuggled under the coverlet and didn't open again until the rattle of my breakfast tray woke me in the morning.

I stretched and sat straighter to receive it across my thighs.

Hannah laid it down, then with surety earned by her many years of service, expressed her displeasure. "'Tis not fitting for you leave me to sleep through thy undressing, my lady. For without your need of me, my status is reduced to below that of the meanest servant in the house undeserving of thy consideration."

I breathed in the scent of hot cocoa and acknowledged my fault. "I know. Forgive me? I was so tired, and my bed called to me. I climbed beneath its covers, my only thought being to do so with the least delay possible."

She sniffed, although her eyes crinkled at the corners. "Very well, my lady, though I do not expect to be so snubbed again."

I dipped my roll, and with normal order restored, asked, "The parcels I purchased yesterday…you have unpacked them?"

She nodded. "I did, but I thought the contents looked a little large for our young earl."

I swallowed my mouthful. "That would be because they are mine. Lay them out for me to dress in, if you would? I have an outing to attend with Lord Francombe, for which I need to be attired as a male."

Her eyebrows shot upwards. "You are donning masculine attire? In public?"

I picked up my bowl of cocoa and prepared to enjoy its contents as much I was Hannah's shocked expression. "Oh, yes. Lord Francombe assures me it is 'de rigueur' that I do so."

She bustled away, muttering under her breath, "Well, His Lordship should know what's what, I suppose…"

I finished my repast, walked to my dressing room and, seeing no steam rising from my water jug, put my finger in and found the contents tepid.

Hannah moved to pick it up. "I will reheat it."

I shook my head. "No. With my full immersion tomorrow, it will do. I partook of no activity yesterday that left me overwarm."

She bobbed a small curtsey to signal her agreement, poured into a porcelain bowl, and sponged my body. Afterwards, I presented my teeth for her to attend to with a fine hickory toothpick, then stepped into my breeches. She put on my shirt, fastened the jabot around my neck with a bow, and buttoned my waistcoat. I shook the ruffles at my sleeve length over my hands then turned this way and that before the mirror, delighting in my freedom from the layers of material that normally swirled around my legs.

Hannah gasped and put her hand over her mouth. "My lady, you may as well walk out of the room naked, so obviously does the material of the breeches cling to your form."

I took another look. "The material is in no way translucent. If it is acceptable for a male to walk the streets attired thus, it should not be considered indecent for a female to do so. There is no more of me on display than there is of them."

Hannah's expression was doubtful, but she forbore to comment and knelt to ease white knee-length silk stockings up my calves then slipped my buckled black leather shoes onto my feet. I smiled at the reflection of my completed outfit and shook my head so my undressed curls undulated down my back.

"I adore my dresses, but I like this also. In future there will be room in my wardrobe for both."

I left my room and skipped down the stairs to see Franny waiting for me at the bottom of them.

He chuckled. "Oh my, I declare I have not seen such a pert satin-clad derrière in quite some while. Come link your arm though mine in the masculine way and try for a little swagger in your walk."

I did so and tried for a confident manner, although I felt somewhat exposed, but I soon began to feel more at ease when no stares of any particular note came my way. We walked arm in arm through the house and down the garden to the wherry pier. I didn't wait for him to hand me down, but freed from the weight of my skirts, leapt aboard the barge to his laugh. He joined me, and the wherryman dipped his pole into the water.

Less than fifteen minutes later, we climbed the steps to an open door, and the footman standing inside it didn't so much as blink in the face of Franny's confident strut of a man familiar with the layout of the palace and the route to Mistress Palmer's apartment.

We climbed the stairs, and the noise level rose, then we entered a room of such opulence my breath caught in my throat. I hesitated on the threshold and tried to take in the intricately embroidered silk panels lining the walls in a riot of colour, candlelight reflecting in the sparkle of crystal chandeliers, and Persian carpets of thick, red lushness on which stood gilded French furniture of such exquisite quality it could have graced Versailles, the palace of the Sun King himself.

Franny urged me forward. More than a dozen gentlemen were ranged around the room, some standing, others taking their ease on sofas or spindle-legged chairs—all of them gazing at the only other lady in the room sitting before her mirror while her maid adjusted her hair, rich chestnut in colour and made more alive by tones of burnished copper running through it. She glanced in the mirror, her bright sapphire eyes finding our reflected entry, and Franny made her a leg.

"The wonderous sight of thine beauty refreshes mine eyes to face the rigors of the day ahead as ever."

I remembered not to curtsey but instead bowed my head, keeping my eyes downcast, as might a gauche, inexperienced young man, fresh to Court. We received her slight nod of acceptance, and Edgeware called to us.

"Well met, Francombe. Come sit beside me and join your adoration of the goddess to mine. Bring the stripling. He can perch on his haunches at our feet."

Lord Exeter laughed. "Nay, Edgeware. 'Tis a pretty lad, and there is more than enough room on my lap for one such as he."

The room laughed with him as the tall, dark figure of the king entered it. I glanced at Mistress Palmer's reflection, and a snap of displeasure entered her eyes.

"You are late."

King Charles smiled at her. "Do not berate me, Barbara. The French Ambassador managed to detain me, and I had the of a devil of a task to send him on his way." He reached into his pocket and pulled the sparkle of precious stones from it. "Still, he left this gift…"

She swivelled on her seat to face him, the perfect bow of her mouth tilting upwards. "You may fasten it on me."

He walked to her and placed the glittering collar around her neck. She turned towards the mirror to admire the reflection of herself wearing it, her good humour restored along with her smile. "Dear Monsieur Dupont. I will not hear a word against him."

I smiled my eyes into Franny's at her abrupt volte-face, and his gleamed his appreciation of the irony back at me. I nudged him in Edgeware's direction and nodded my intention to sit with Exeter. Franny took his place while I wiggled my rear in between Exeter and an elderly gentleman I faintly recognised from last evening, sitting beside him on the sofa.

Exeter lifted my hand as if to kiss it. "Such an unexpected pleasure to see you again so soon after I wished for it to be so, my lay…"

I pressed my index finger to his lips to shush him.

He smiled at his near faux pas and continued. "My lad. Your dealing of the cards was masterful."

His companion, to my other side, peered shortsightedly in our direction. "A lad dealt the cards at your table last night? I could have sworn it was a pretty blonde female dressed all in gold and whatnot."

I exchanged a laughing glance with Exeter then looked away to find the king's eyes, gleaming with amused comprehension, focused upon our sofa. I grinned my own enjoyment back at him then turned away.

Mistress Palmer, too long out of the limelight, I presumed, rapped her fan against her dressing table and stood. "The park awaits us, I believe?"

Glasses that had contained sherry-wine were set down, and the room rose to its feet. Mistress Palmer stood and plumped her skirts. Exeter offered me his arm, and I tucked mine through it. We waited until the king led Mistress Palmer past us, and his eyes paused on my face when he did so, which I counted as a step forward as we sauntered, two by two, down the stairs behind them.

Franny unlinked his arm from Edgeware's, stepped to one side, and captured my hand to stand with him when we reached the bottom of them, leaving Edgeware no choice but to walk on with Exeter, and he made his feelings known at having to do so by way of an icy glare in my direction. I waited with Franny until the king's party passed from our view, then we left the palace by way of the river door we had arrived at.

"Your beau is less than pleased by your leaving him?"

He shrugged his unconcern. "He was already out of sorts with me for refusing to divulge your name last evening despite his urgings, but if he knew me better than he believes he does, he would know I am not a man inclined to dance to the tune of any other's making bar my own."

I jumped into the wherry. "He mistakes your good-nature for weakness?"

Franny sat beside me, and the wherryman pushed off from the jetty.

"I may have been over enamoured at the start of our friendship as to lead him to think me compliant. I will endeavour to correct that opinion, but if my true nature does not suit him, our ways will part."

I squeezed his hand. "I will hope for a happy resolution for you."

He smiled and tucked my arm through his. "So, that aside, your conclusions having viewed Mistress Palmer?"

"She is beauty personified and charming when pleased, but the attention she receives has led her to become haughty and mayhap arrogant. If her rooms have been decorated to her design, she adores bright colours, so I will present myself in opposing contrast. Yesterday, King Charles viewed me in gold. Tomorrow, for my Presentation, my gown is silver. I shall wear only those two colours for the remainder of my stay in the capital and keep my demeanour flirtatious and light."

He laughed. "Excellent. His letter to you is already in the bag. I know it!"

The wherryman punted on until Franny called to him.

"We will alight at the next jetty."

I looked, for it was not the one at the Melville residence. "Our outing is not at an end?"

"No, my angel. We are going to visit several ale houses of my acquaintance to kick up some noise then eat a large, bloody steak for our supper before we stagger home."

I grinned my delight. "An ale house, Franny? Really?"

He smacked my rear as I stood to disembark the wherry. "Out with you, young sir. You require a little beer and red meat to put some flesh on your bones."

I jumped from the barge with a giggle, then threaded my arm through his. "Outrageous, Franny! The poor boatman did not know where to put his face!"

He laughed. "No, but we have made our mark. Wherrymen gossip, and their fares hear them when they do, therein, news of our antics will become known to add to the fun."

I smiled, and we walked on, the malodorous whiff of gutter and midden becoming more apparent the farther we moved away from the river along an alley lined to each side with a motley mismatch of timber-framed dwellings. A dingy building, four stories high and so crookedly built it leaned on its nearest neighbour for support, hove into view. Franny stopped before it, unlatched its door, and ducked his head under a low lintel, tugging me in after him. The stench from the tallow dip lights caught in my throat, and my eyes watered as I entered.

I coughed. "Jesu, Franny! You men find this atmosphere convivial, do you?"

He winked. "Yes, dearest. Look around at the quality of the doxies and lightskirts for hire. If we do not come across at least the Duke of York or William Chiffinch, the king's pimp-master general in one of these establishments before we return home tonight, I will hold myself surprised."

My own surprise snorted down my nose. "At least?"

He laughed. "Your education is sadly lacking, my lad. King Charles does not restrict himself to only the enjoyment of Mistress Palmer's charms and is not above putting in an appearance to partake of the entertainment on offer, though he leaves it to Chiffinch to negotiate the price. Now let us order something thick and brown in a tankard. If you find it too noisome you can just pretend to drink it." He beckoned a wench holding a tray.

She swayed towards us, the neckline of her blouse low enough to show the blush of her nipple. "Sirs?"

Franny placed two copper pennies on her tray. "A tankard a piece and be quick about it."

She bobbed a curtsey, leaning forward as she did so to give us more than just a glimpse of her breasts. I looked past her and, appearing through veils of hanging smoke, small groups of men in twos, threes, or fours supped from their tankards, laughing or in earnest conversation, and tucked in the corner, a man with a serving girl sitting on his lap, his fingers exploring the delights normally hidden beneath her skirt.

The bar wench returned with our ale. Franny passed me mine. I sipped and found the drink bitter but not as unpalatable as I had imagined it would be, so chugged male-style then wiped my foam moustache across the back of my hand.

Franny grinned. "That's the way, lad."

We downed our beer, moved on to the next ale house, and by the time we entered the fourth, the sun had been replaced by a full moon, and I found the smoke and the smell of beer within had ceased to bother me very much at all. I took a deep draught from my tankard. Franny draped his arm over my shoulders and leaned closer to my ear.

"My sweet, look to the side of me."

I did so, saw a man, and released my mirth as I recognised his distinctive height and long, dark-haired curls in the midst of a boisterous crowd.

"Oh, Jesu! I thought you were jesting with me earlier."

At my gales of laughter, several heads turned in our direction, including the king's. Franny dropped his tankard, clasped my waist, then threw me over his shoulder with a loud smack on my rear and announced, "That's quite enough ale for you. Home with us, my lad."

My own tankard hit the floor, and I laughed louder. He carried me from the ale house and kissed his cheek when he set me on my feet outside the door.

"That was such fun," I said.

He smiled his satisfaction. "Our game progresses in fine style. Shall we seek us our supper?"

With the quantity of dark brew swirling around in my stomach, I found myself nothing loathe, so nodded my agreement, hiccupped, and put my arm through his. We walked on, and my head became woozy in the night air rather than refreshed to be out of the smoking tallow.

"I do not believe I could manage to sup any more of the dark brew, though."

By the light of the moon, he peered at my face. "You do look a little green around the gills, dearest one. Shall we, instead, disappear from sight and return home so you may digest something a little lighter than bloody meat?"

"If you please, yes."

He supported me with an arm around my waist until we reached the wherry pier, then again up the stairs to my room. Hannah was sitting in her chair mending my stockings when he escorted me through the door and jumped to her feet as he assisted me to a sofa.

"Perhaps some soup, bread, and cheese for your mistress' supper, if you would?"

She bobbed her curtsey. "Very well, my lord."

Franny sat with me until she returned, then kissed my hand goodnight. "With Presentation on the morrow, it is no bad thing our festivities have ended early. I will await the sight of your glory in the Tapestry room to partake of a glass of sherry-wine at noon."

He left.

Hannah removed my clothes, put a fresh smock on me, then led me to my bed, and I eagerly ate every scrap of the supper on the tray she laid across my lap. I snuggled under the covers once it was removed then drifted into a dream-filled sleep where the near-black eyes of a dark-haired man turned inexplicably to warm green, and firmer lips replaced the softness of those pressed against my own to my sigh.

Chapter Five

I woke in the morning, thankfully clear of head but with a raging thirst. Hannah brought a pitcher of icy water drawn from the deep well in the kitchen to accompany my breakfast. I drank until I'd emptied it and felt revived for doing so.

She took the cup and pitcher from my tray, leaving my hot cocoa and rolls and bustled away. "The footmen will arrive with thy bath shortly, so

I will close the bedroom door against their catching sight of your undress."

I finished my cocoa and rolls when she did so then relaxed against my pillows until she returned and announced, "Your bath awaits thee, my lady."

I put my feet to the floor and saw a steaming full tub in my dressing room. Hannah removed my smock, and I sank down in its linen-lined depths with a sigh of pleasure as hot water engulfed me. She handed me a small bar of lye soap infused with lemon balm and added a few drops of rose-scented oil to the water. I passed the bar over my skin then tipped my head and doused my hair. She worked a little soap through its length, rinsed it with a jug of clear, warm water, then held out my winding sheet.

Patted dry, the damp lengths of my hair brushed through and my skin powdered, I walked to my sitting room wearing a loose robe belted at the waist and penned a few lines to Bonnie while my bath was emptied bucket by bucket out of the window to the footmen's cries of "'Ware below!" and the tub removed. I returned to my dressing room when the door to my suite shut behind them.

Hannah ran her fingers through my hair. "'Tis dry enough for the heat of the curling irons to set your ringlets, I believe."

I nodded. She removed my robe, replaced it with my chemise, and gartered stockings, then I sat before the mirror.

"I have decided to make my mark by appearing in only gold and silver for the length of my stay. During my absence today, visit the Royal Exchange, purchase petticoats of gold and silver net to alter the appearance of the two gowns I possess, and set as many seamstresses as will be necessary on notice that I require at least half a dozen new gowns to be created for me in the days ahead."

She smiled at my reflection and applied the curling irons. "A choice as will suit thy fair colouring to best advantage, my lady. Shall I request they attend you here with their pattern books on the morrow?"

"Directly after I have broken my fast, if you would."

I held still until my hair was dressed then stepped into the fullness of my flounced underskirt, and Hannah settled the shimmering folds of my gown over it. She fastened the silver buttons at my back but did not gather and lift the material to reveal any of my petticoat, given the formality of the occasion. A separate jewel chest contained my mother's diamonds, and I opened it, smiling at my memory of her wearing them — beautiful and lustrously alive, like the stones themselves, before a cough and blood-spotted handkerchief foretold her final fate.

I handed Hannah the tiara—a half-circlet of two hundred sparkling, facet-cut jewels that rose in an arch to frame a central pear-drop of such a size as to outshine the rest. She fixed it to my hair, added a pair of drop earrings, and picked up a dazzling neck collar from the box which I rejected.

"No, not that piece. It detracts the eye away from the neckline of my gown. The encrusted bangles, two on each arm, if you please, and Mama's betrothal ring to complete the set."

She placed them on me, blackened my lashes, and added a little additional blush to my lips. I tilted my head this way and that in the mirror. Hannah eased my feet into satin court shoes with a two-inch heel and handed me an ivory stick and silk fan. I took a final look at my shimmering reflection, thanked her for her dressing of me, then left my suite and dipped my curtsey before my godmama when I entered the Tapestry room.

She inclined her head. "You look radiant, Emma."

I straightened, took in her plumed headdress above a sumptuous gown of burnt-orange velvet overlaid with the finest Brussels lace, her ensemble adorned with jewels of amber and topaz set in gold, and acknowledged her rising well in advance of her accustomed hour for my benefit. "Your Grace, I cannot thank you enough for the honour you pay to me today."

She waved off my compliment but seemed pleased to have received it by her smile. "Nonsense, child. It is nothing but my pleasure to present you."

Franny stepped forward and bowed, his blue eyes full of laughter. "Shining goddess, I am overcome…"

"As you were last evening when you so shamefully manhandled my person?"

My godmother tapped his wrist with her fan as he straightened. "Franny, you did not?"

He smirked. "Yes, Mama, I did, but Emma was at fault. Dressed as a boy, she supped too well at the ale house, so I picked her up, slapped her rear, and carried her out of the place."

The duchess snapped open her fan and wafted it in front of her face. "Franny, I swear you will be the death of me. Thank the Lord you have a younger brother more alive to his responsibility to marry and produce offspring than you."

Franny let out his laugh. "Yes, Mama, but Richard doesn't amuse you as I do, though I am grateful to him for staying at home in the country with m'father to manage the estate—and more so, for sparing me the task of siring an heir, for which he, along with his wife and spawn, are welcome to the lot when I depart this life."

She smiled and closed her fan. "Then all is well."

Franny beckoned a footman, and he moved forward with brimming stemmed glasses on a tray, another following behind him carrying a dish of dainty mutton pasties in one hand and a platter of quince tartlets in the other. We sipped and ate several of the pies apiece to ward off any hunger pangs during the afternoon, then set down our glasses, and Franny offered his mama one arm and me the other.

The carriage and four waited at the portico, and we travelled to Whitehall by land rather than water in respect of the duchess' distaste for the rocking motion of a barge. The coach pulled up outside the Banqueting House. Franny handed us out and led us to join the throng making their way into the sumptuous double-height hall to attend the king's levee.

Inside, the crowd hoping for a minute or two of his time, milled around beneath Ruben's glorious Renaissance paintings set into gilded panels on the ceiling, awaiting his arrival. I looked about me to see who I recognised now I was able to match two dozen or more names to their faces and saw, in the center the room, Mistress Palmer surrounded by various courtiers vying for her attention, including her cousin, George Villiers, the Duke of Buckingham, and Sir Charles Berkeley, Keeper of the Privy Purse.

Behind the group I spied Lord Exeter in close conversation with the poet, Fleetwood Sheppard, while beside me my godmother and Franny were bowing or nodding at their own respective acquaintances, including Viscount Edgeware who glanced at me coolly then frowned, his gaze resting on the glittering stones of my tiara. They widened slightly as his eyes moved to the duchess standing at my side.

He walked forward and made his bow before her. "Your Grace. I am charmed to see you here. Francombe, delighted as ever, and…?"

She acknowledged his good wishes with a smile and introduced me. "My goddaughter, Lady Emma…"

Edgeware bowed his respects to me without waiting for the completion of my title, but I caught the piercing glare he sent towards Franny, guessed the meaning of it, and giggled. "Franny, you didn't?"

Franny's eyes sparkled. "Of course I did, dearest heart. Following his delight at seeing you in my company at the masquerade, how could I resist the jest that I knew not your name because…"

I laughed and finished his sentence for him. "You didn't quite hear it when you paid for my company?"

His mama smacked his wrist with her fan then opened it to cover her amusement, but Edgeware's response to Franny's smoking of him became lost as a door opened to one side of the throne and King Charles sauntered into the room without ceremony, three of the small dogs named for him gambolling around his heels.

He sat. The Comptroller of his household closed the door behind him and nodded towards my godmother. She took my hand and led me forward to stand before the throne. The king looked at my face, his lips tilting into a smile of recognition.

My godmother dipped only the half-curtsey required of her rank and said, "Sire, may I present my goddaughter, Lady Emma Bonneville, Countess of Summerly?"

His smile widened, and he offered me his hand as he answered her. "Willingly, dear lady."

I sank into a full Court curtsey as was his due, then knelt before my Sovereign to pay homage by kissing his coronation ring. I moved my lips over it, then experienced the charm that had caught the country's heart since his Restoration. He stood, assisted me to rise, and brushed his mouth across my knuckles, the soft hair of his moustache tickling my skin.

"You are welcome, Lady Emma. It is our pleasure to see you here."

My heart thumped at his touch. He released my hand and turned to my godmother.

"Your Grace. We see too little of you at Court. You must leave your card evenings and join us more often."

She smiled. "You are kind, Sire, but you have no need of an old dame at your entertainments. I gift you my goddaughter in my place. She will add to your enjoyment rather than take from it."

His gaze warmed on my face. "I believe she will."

My public introduction to him complete, we stepped three paces blindly backwards so as not to turn our backs on the throne, then took two paces sideways which released us from our obligation. Franny appeared beside us, a footman with wine-filled silver goblets on a tray following behind him.

"Mama, you were magnificent. Heart of my heart, I swear the room gasped at your shimmering beauty."

I kissed my fingers at him for the compliment, took a goblet, then noticed Edgeware standing behind him.

He raised his wine at me and drawled in the faintly sneering tones I was fast coming to detest. "So, not just Lady Emma, but also the Countess of Summerly. Forgive my not recognising your quality on any earlier occasion, but you play your part so well as to be indistinguishable from any common lightskirt available for hire."

I shrugged my bland-faced indifference at his opinion of me and returned to him in equal measure. "Do not trouble yourself, my lord. A man whose only attraction to feminine company is in his ability to pay for it, is not likely to recognise anything else."

His eyes grew colder at my riposte and icier still when I turned my shoulder on him in favour of smiling at Lord Exeter who arrived before me in full flow.

"Beauteous lady, in your gown of gold you outshone the sun, dressed in silver, you eclipse every star in the heavens."

I offered my hand for his kiss, then felt several small crunchy tremors at my feet. I picked up the hem of my skirt and saw a miniature black-and-tan spaniel with its teeth buried in the heel of my shoe, its long curly haired ears flapping to each side of its head as it gnawed with gusto. I handed Exeter my goblet, scooped it up, noted its sex, and kissed his little black nose.

"You are a scallywag, sir. Between you and Franny, I swear I shall not have any decent footwear left to my name." The pup licked my chin and answered me by way of a wag of his tail. I set him down and giggled when he trotted off, cocked his leg, and peed over Edgeware's own shoe.

He nudged the little dog away with his foot and glared at me.

I laughed louder, and the king's voice sounded behind me.

"My pets amuse you as they do me?" he asked.

Exeter made his bow to him then melted away and I smiled my agreement.

"He is a charming little scamp, and 'tis only a shoe."

King Charles returned my smile. "It is indeed our pleasure to meet you here, Lady Emma—a new jewel to adorn our Court, although I believe, mayhap, I encountered your young brother yesterday?"

An unmistakable glint of interest in my person glittered in his eyes, and I responded lightly.

"Mayhap you did, for he is a naughty lad, and there is no saying where he will turn up next."

He took my hand and kissed the pulse of my wrist. "I look forward to deepening my acquaintance with the both of you."

My breath caught at the heat that tingled between my thighs, although I schooled my face not to show it as I dipped my curtsey. "As will I."

I straightened. He walked on to exchange a few words with other guests in the room, then Edgeware's cold drawl set my nerves on edge.

"Do not take the compliment to yourself. He will forget your very existence in about three more paces when he catches sight of Mistress Palmer."

I didn't deign to even so much as look at him and acknowledge he had spoken but answered the empty air in front of me. "Do feel free to follow his lead, and I will return the same towards you."

His soft laugh was low enough to reach my ears only. "No, madam. You have challenged me, and I am not a man to back down before such provocation. When I take you to wife, you will learn better than to do so, I swear it."

The ridiculousness of his statement tickled my ribs, even while I wondered what assurances my uncle must have uttered to lead him to believe that my compliance in the matter was no more than mere formality. The urge to laugh in his face and dismiss his pretensions outright rose to my lips, but I resisted the temptation to do so until I was in a less crowded space.

Instead, I turned and opened my fan with a bored sigh. "I do believe you have missed your calling, sir. Drury Lane surely beckons to one so skilled in the performance of unnecessary melodrama, but pray, do not let me detain you and deprive the room of your company."

I picked up my skirt, turned my back on him, and smiled at Lord Exeter when he stepped forward and reoffered me my goblet.

"Star of stars gifted to us from the heavens above, your wine?" he said.

I took it and sipped. Lord Saltash walked up to us.

"The devil must be on Edgeware's shoulder. He just pushed past me without so much as a by your leave," he said.

I smiled a smile of demure innocence. "Mayhap, because the king's pet has just pissed on him?"

Lord Exeter chuckled and toasted me with his wine. "Well, from my observation, if not the spaniel then someone else, most assuredly, just has."

I shrugged my unconcern, then Franny stepped closer and offered me his arm.

"Come, lovely creature. Let us return home ahead of your admirers. The party cannot begin in the absence of the one in whose honour it is being held."

I curtsied my temporary farewell to Exeter and Saltash then left the audience chamber as I had arrived at it, escorted by Franny with my godmother to his other side.

She smiled as the carriage pulled away. "Excellent, Emma. King Charles sought you out after your Presentation."

I squeezed Franny's hand. "Yes, but I also managed to offend Viscount Edgeware. He seems to believe our future marriage is a certainty, the misunderstanding of which I will lay at Uncle John's door, but he was rather arrogant over the matter, so…"

Franny returned the pressure of my hand. "You disabused him of the notion?"

I nodded. "Not as an outright denial with so many persons standing around us, but…yes."

Godmama huffed. "I will say it again. John is a menace. He interferes in the business of others, ignorant and without knowledge, thinking only of his own advantage. Franny, soothe your friend, if you will? With his title and status, there must be other females who would appreciate the honour he is offering to give him, no need to fix his attentions on one who does not wish for them."

Franny smiled at her then winked at me. "Be assured, Mama. Of a certainty, I shall pour forth my best endeavours to persuade him."

She opened her fan, wafted it, and snorted. "Franny!"

I swatted his arm and joined my laugh to hers.

The carriage pulled up. We processed to the ballroom to take our places inside it, and after an hour of dipping and inclining my head to a succession of names I would never remember, Franny offered me one arm and his mama the other. We walked into the midst of the throng, and the musicians struck up the opening notes of the first dance. Earl Rochester claimed my hand, though I noted from the glance he sent towards Franny where his interest lay, and it was not with me.

We moved through the steps of a stately Pavane, exchanged partners for the Allemande, then again for a Minuet, and at no time during the evening did the proceedings descend into a romp. The ballroom emptied around two. I thanked my godmother for hosting the party in my honour while Franny filled a platter with morsels of supper I'd so far had no time to taste, then escorted me upstairs.

He set the food on a table as I signed to Hannah to remove my tiara which seemed to weigh twice as much as it had when she'd placed it on my head. I sat and sighed my relief when she lifted it to Franny's smile.

"You were ravishing, my angel. Have you had any thoughts on when you wish to hold your Grande Toilette?"

I selected an onion tartlet from my plate. "Perhaps, two days hence? I have seamstresses attending me in the morning to refresh my choice of gowns according to the colour scheme I have devised."

He nodded. "Then on the morrow I will make myself busy around Town and set up the buzz of your doing so. Shall we meet again in the Tapestry room before dinner and exchange news of our progress?"

I offered my free hand for his kiss. "That will be delightful, my Adonis. Adieu, until we meet again."

He brushed his lips across my knuckles, and I munched gratefully on my late-night repast after he left me. Once I'd emptied my plate, Hannah assisted me into bed, and I drifted off to sleep wondering on whom the king's sensuous mouth was currently being employed, accompanied by a sharp stab of dislike at the thought of Hugo Fitzwilliam doing anything at all similar with someone other than me.

I dressed in a loose robe in the morning then sat on the sofa in my sitting room while Hannah descended the stairs to discover whether the seamstresses had arrived, but when the door reopened, it was not her but a footman with a letter addressed to me bearing a waxed imprint of 'HF'. I took it, broke the seal, and read…

My lady,

I trust my missive finds you well and entrust to you the knowledge of the quarter-end receipts having been safely garnered. An investment opportunity has arisen for them. I will bring the funds required to London under armed escort within the next sennight in lieu of your approval of the scheme on offer. For your reassurance, in my absence from Summerly, I have secured other items of value in the house, including the surplus revenue remaining from previous quarters, away from the property.

As ever, I am yours to command,
Fitzwilliam. H.

Happiness that I would be in Hugo's company sooner than expected fizzed in my belly, and I smiled at our shared secret of the strong boxes now safely locked behind the iron gates of the icehouse my uncle did not know existed.

Hannah returned as I refolded the vellum, and I surveyed the pattern books while she gave the seamstresses my measurements. I selected six new gowns, sharing the commission between them without quibbling over the price, so with promises they had a sufficiency of girls on hand to welcome the work, they departed with their assurances that the first of my dresses would be with me in no more than three days.

The rest of the morning I whiled away with Hannah attending to necessary details of my personal care—trimming my nails with a paring knife, plucking stray hairs from where they should not be, and applying lotions to soften my skin. I talked of what would be required for my Grande Toilette while nibbling on a platter of fresh fruit as she worked, and shortly after one of the clock, a tap on the dressing room door signalled the arrival of a pageboy bearing a message.

"If it please thee, my lady. Lord Saltash awaits below with his sister and wonders if you would wish to accompany them on an outing to the Privy Garden at Whitehall?"

I smiled my pleasure at receiving the invitation. "Indeed, I would. Return that as my answer, then show them up to my sitting room and serve some honey wine while I ready myself."

Hannah, so experienced at her job, had moved into action while I spoke and placed the curling irons in the fire.

I turned to her when the door closed. "With as much speed and as little fuss as may be managed, my gold gown with the new over-petticoat of silver, if you would."

She nodded and removed the garments from the clothes press. I sat and pointed my toes for her to roll on my stockings then stood, stepped into my outfit, and retook my seat for her to apply my cosmetics and set a dozen ringlets into my hair. Her deft fingers worked quickly, and in less than twenty minutes, she pinned bunches of silver ribbons to the ringlets gathered to each side of my head. I turned back and forth in front of the looking glass after she placed my shoes on my feet and was delighted with the result.

"My dress is sufficiently changed as not to appear the same as it did before, and the ribbons in my hair please me more than would my hat. I thank you."

She nodded. "Your beauty is easy to dress, my lady, as was your mother's when I was permitted to do such a thing before the strictures of the Interregnum."

A band squeezed tight around my heart. "Mama had some years of happiness before merriment and joy were banned, did she not? My memory does not play me false?"

Her lips tilted to a wistful smile. "That she did. Your remembrance is true, though you were younger than George when it was so."

I squeezed her hand. "I'm glad. It comforts me."

Hannah returned the pressure of my hand, and the murmur of voices recalled us to the present. She bobbed her curtsy and opened the dressing room door. I walked to the sitting room. A pretty brunette sat beside Lord Saltash on the sofa.

He stood and bowed. "May I present m'sister, Lady Helen?"

I smiled. "I would be delighted."

Having already named her before she'd risen to make her curtsey, he looked at a loss for a minute but recovered himself with a small cough. "Yes… Well… Golden goddess before whom the midday orb blushes with shame…"

His sister's giggle cut off the flow of his words. "Oh, Salty, no. Not that one. I told you it would set me off if you uttered it."

My smile widened as I glanced at her. "Salty?"

She grinned. "Since we were young, and he practices on me all the flowery phrases he thinks will impress a lady."

I laughed, and she joined me to Lord Saltash's theatrically huffed, "If you ladies have quite finished smoking me, may we depart?"

We smirked at each other and accompanied him from the house.

The sun warmed my shoulders as we walked, and the birds chirped as if the season was spring not autumn when we joined the crowd at Whitehall strolling along the paths intersecting the grass squares of the Privy Garden, each of which had contained a fine carved statue before they had had been smashed to pieces for being ungodly, graven images during the Interregnum.

Lady Helen sighed. "Unseasonable it may be, but this weather is heavenly, is it not?"

I agreed, and we walked on, bowing and nodding our respects to those persons we recognised, the gardens more now busy thoroughfare than the private pleasure park of their inception for those making their way between the haphazard assortment of buildings that comprised the Palace of Whitehall. I returned the smile of one of the players who had sat at my card table, Madam Blake, then spied Franny arm in arm with Edgeware a few yards ahead.

Franny kissed his fingers to me when we reached him. "Sweetest of angels, mine heart aches for not having caught sight of your perfection this day."

I exchanged an amused smile with Lady Helen at the fulsome floweriness of his words, then responded in kind. "My lord, I swear I can scarce draw breath when you speak to me thus."

She giggled, and Franny turned his attention towards her and Lord Saltash as Edgeware bowed to me and drawled, "Last evening, Viscount Francombe brought to my notice a possible misunderstanding between us. If your uncle has not as yet expressed his wish for our future marriage in clear enough terms, I would beg your pardon for presuming he had?"

My hackles rose at the words *as yet*, but for Franny's sake, I swallowed the acidic retort on the tip of my tongue in favour of a more neutral response. "My pardon is freely given, my lord. However, so the matter is not mistaken between us again, my uncle's wishes are his alone. I am in no way beholden to them."

He frowned. "You believe you, a mere female, can gainsay a duke?"

I stared my defiance into his eyes.

His face tightened. "We shall see about that, madam. We shall see." He turned away. "Francombe, come. We are bidden to partake of our dinner with the king in Mistress Palmer's rooms shortly, I believe?"

Franny nodded, made his farewells to Lady Helen and Saltash, then kissed my cheek. "My apologies, dearest heart. I will seek you on the morrow, for although I cannot be in the Tapestry room tonight, I promise to be the first adoring attendee at your Grande Toilette come the morning."

I kissed him back, then for Lady Helen's entertainment and to cock a snook at Edgeware, trilled, "Oh, my Adonis. I can scarce wait for you to come find me in my bed."

Lady Helen snorted, Franny and Lord Saltash laughed, and Edgeware glowered.

"Francombe, let us not keep the king waiting, if you please."

They walked away, and Lady Helen gazed after them. "Viscount Edgeware appears a man of little good humour?"

Saltash patted her hand. "With a fond mama and seven sisters, four in front and three behind, he does not do well with females not inclined to fawn over his person. When among men, he is good company, and a bride of sufficiently robust attitude will smooth his rough edges and ensure his presence is welcome by all."

Lady Helen tucked her arm through her brother's, looking as doubtful as I myself felt about his pronouncement. I took his other arm, and we returned to my godmother's house to partake of our own dinner and enjoy an evening of cards.

Chapter Six

I tripped up the stairs to my rooms shortly after one of the clock and dismissed Hannah to her own bed in the servant's hall after she undressed me. "Wake me no later than seven on the morrow. We have much to do to ensure I am presentable before I am supposedly awoken by my early morning callers."

She placed my nightstick on the table beside my bed then tamped the wicks of the other candles standing about the room. "As it please thee, my lady. Sleep well."

I yawned and lay my head on the pillow. "And you." I closed my eyes to a small frisson of fear that not even Franny would be at my Grande Toilette, then reposed my trust in him, Exeter, and Saltash, at least, to attend and fell asleep.

Hannah woke me in good time, but I managed less than a third of my breakfast when nervous excitement caused my dish of cocoa to shake as I raised it to my lips. I abandoned my tray, saw to my personal needs in the closet, then walked to the dressing room. Hannah sponged and talcumed my body, curled my hair, made up my face, then dressed me in a clean under-smock. I climbed back into bed and reclined on my pillows. She straightened the covers before laying my petticoat, dress, and stockings over a chair with my shoes beneath it.

The door to my bedroom opened, and Franny walked in, wonderfully attired in red satin with a footman, one step behind him, carrying a tray of stemmed glasses filled with sherry-wine.

I smiled my relief at the sight of him. "You look dressed for a ball, though 'tis before nine in the morn."

He sat on the side of my bed. "Of course, sweet one. Nothing less will do. Due homage must be paid to the most beautiful angel it has ever been my privilege to behold if she herself is ready to receive several lords and a duke of the royal blood?"

I squeaked. "You have secured the king's brother?"

Franny winked. "At the very least, but now close your eyes, for I believe I hear the first footfall on the stairs."

I squeezed his hand and pretended sleep to his sighed, "Oh, my lords, step closer. Our goddess stirs, I believe."

I fluttered my lashes and opened my eyes. "Oh, goodness! I am quite overcome to see you gentlemen here at my waking."

"Beautiful lady, I am honoured…"

"Star of Heaven…"

"Smile on me, wonderous angel, I beg thee…"

"Golden goddess before whom the midday orb blushes with shame…"

I smiled my appreciation at Lord Saltash for his ribbing me and offered him my hand. "Such eloquence, as I can scarce believe you dared utter the words, my lord. Would you care to assist me to rise?"

He expressed his happiness at being chosen to do so and escorted me over to Hannah to gasps of admiration from the men in the room at the sight of my bare feet and ankles showing beneath my smock. The footman offered the glasses around. I stepped into a gold net petticoat, and as Hannah fastened it, the Duke of York walked into the room.

Her eyes widened at the sight of a royal prince. I dipped my curtsey to his smiled, "I see rumour does not lie, beautiful lady."

"I am honoured, Your Highness."

Hannah recovered her composure and dressed me in my gown, only to lose it again when King Charles entered the room. "Od's fish, brother. You think to steal a march on me by arriving beforehand?"

Prince James picked up a glass of wine with a shrug. "'Tis only fair I do so when all other natural advantage belongs to yourself."

I trod lightly on Hannah's foot, and she closed her mouth which had fallen into a round 'O'. I sat. She picked up my stocking, and the king walked closer.

"'Twill avail you nothing, for I am here now, so the honour is mine if the lady permits?"

My cheeks heated, and I nodded my acceptance, untrusting of my voice not to betray my nerves if I spoke. Hannah's hand shook when she offered him my stocking.

He took it and smiled into her eyes. "Do not tremble, good woman. 'Tis only I, Old Roly."

She emitted a soft squawk and released my stocking, and I well-nigh joined her as the king sank to his knees before me.

"Sweet lady, if I may?"

I looked into his near-black eyes and, my heart racing, lifted the skirt of my dress up to my knees to various sighs.

"Exquisite…"

"A calf of utter perfection…"

"Aphrodite would tear at her locks in jealous rage…"

I pointed my toes. The king placed my stocking onto my foot then eased it up my leg with his long, slender fingers, pausing to stroke the sensitive crease behind my knee before meting out the same treatment to my other leg. My garters he fastened with practiced smoothness, and once he had secured them, he slid on my shoes.

"There you are ready…mayhap for an outing in my company?"

I swallowed hard for the wetness between my legs at his touch but managed to keep my voice steady, "As it please thee, Sire, yes."

He stood and offered me his hand. I put mine into the warmth of his, and the gentlemen in the room formed up behind us as they had for Mistress Palmer.

He looked over his shoulder. "Rochester. Buckingham. I believe you, along with Francombe, Exeter, and Saltash have another toilette to attend at eleven whilst I am *unavoidably* detained by matters of state?"

They nodded, and King Charles returned his attention to me. My visitors followed us out of the room and down the stairs. Several mounts held by their grooms snorted their impatience at being required to stand outside the house.

He paused at the head of a broad-shouldered chestnut with a saddle rug of royal purple, beside which stood a dappled-grey mare similarly dressed, and gazed into my eyes. "You will accept my mount?"

My heart thumped as I took his meaning and I responded in a similar manner. "Indeed, I will, with every expectation of enjoying the ride."

His eyes reflected his satisfaction at my answer. He assisted me into the saddle of the mare then threw his leg over the back of his own steed. "We shall ride to the kennels at Whitehall."

I took the reins from the groom. The king turned his horse in the direction of the palace, and

I rode alongside him, his retinue two-by-two behind us, with the grooms running at a fast trot at our flanks. The lords he had named peeled away as we entered the palace by way of the Holbein Gate. We pulled up at an outbuilding, and the biscuity, milky smell of pups tickled my nose.

King Charles handed me down, escorted me inside, and I laughed with pleasure when I saw several bitches nesting with their offspring. I sank to my knees and picked up a male with more black colouring in his coat than tan, worrying his mother's nipples. The pup nuzzled my neck, his tiny pink tongue lapping hopefully.

The king crouched beside me. "You like him?"

I kissed its nose. "He is adorable."

"Then he is yours. He is near ready to leave his mother and find a new home."

I smiled my delight at the gift. "I may have him? Truly?"

He nodded, and I cuddled the tiny creature to my breast.

"But you must also pick another," he said. "His breed crave company, and he will be unhappy without a friend."

My happiness increased at the thought of two pups, one each for George and Bonnie, so I visited the other litters and set my pup down close by them to judge who would be a suitable companion for him. Most ignored him, busy on their mother's teats, until a pup of opposing colouring, more tan than black, turned from its mother to lick his face. I picked it up, found it to be female, and the king laughed.

"A perfect match. I believe I will use the method in future to decide which dog and bitch should breed." He beckoned to a kennel lad. "Bring two lengths of ribbon to mark the lady's choice."

The lad looked at a loss for a moment then removed the one tethering his hair at the nape of his neck, cut it in half with a small bladed knife, and held them out. The king took the pieces and gave my pups a collar each.

I smiled at the lad. "I thank you. I will make sure you receive another to replace it if you will tell me your name."

He blushed bright crimson. "Thankee, my lady. 'Tis Will the younger, as it please thee."

I nodded, and the king offered me his hand.

"Your pups will be ready in a sennight, but now, much as I may wish it different, I must order an escort to see you home, for Clarendon will be snapping at my heels should I tarry longer."

I stood with a smile as I pictured his starchy Lord High Chancellor doing so. "Poor man. Let us not put him to the trouble."

King Charles urged me closer and murmured, "But you will sup with me this evening?"

I nodded.

"Come to me by way of the water at six of the clock. The wherryman will bring you to the king's door. Suitable escort will be waiting to show you to my private rooms."

My heart raced at the prospect, that at his hands, my penetration might be more pleasure than a means to an end. "I shall be there."

He planted a soft kiss on my cheek then stepped away and looked at his remaining retinue standing gossiping to each side of the door. "James, with me. If I must face Clarendon's strictures, so must you. Berkeley, escort the countess back to the Melville residence, and the rest of you have my leave to stay or go as you please."

Those unnamed did not avail themselves of his offer to go about their own business, and as the king left the building with the fast, long-legged stride for which he was renowned when not walking with a lady, they hastened after him at a half-run.

I turned towards Berkeley. "Sir Charles, do not feel obligated to stay behind. I am familiar with my way home. A kennel lad could accompany me just as well."

His well worn, puffy face that belied he had attained little more than thirty years in age creased into a mock grimace of pain. "Spare me Clarendon's hand-wringing, I beg? 'Tis not a pretty sight."

I laughed and dipped him a half-curtsey. "As you wish, my lord."

We left the pups behind in their breeding shed, abandoned our horses to the care of their grooms, and walked to the Melville residence talking of the productions being performed at the theatre. I thanked him for his company when we arrived but did not linger, impatient to seek my godmother's advice on a matter nagging at the back of my mind. I enquired of the young page in the hall where she might be found, and he pointed me in the direction of her sitting room. I found her drinking a dish of tea when I entered it.

She smiled and beckoned. "Come and sit with me. Tell me the detail of your Grande Toilette? I have been in such a twitch all this day since I received word Prince James had arrived to attend you, shortly followed by the king himself."

I settled myself in the chair opposite her, happy she had raised the very subject I wished to converse with her about. The maid set a dish of tea before me and a plate of small cakes on the table between us. The duchess dismissed all the servants with a wave of her hand.

I ate a sponge finger and sipped as they left the room, then set down my dish. "Franny was magnificent in spreading word of my toilette taking place. Many lords attended along with the prince and the king…" I blushed at the remembrance. "The king put my stockings, garters, and shoes on me, then invited me to ride out with him. He took me to see his pups and gifted me a pair…"

Her eyebrows rose. "Well done, Emma. King Charles allows his pets to leave his care less often than he hands out titles and jewels."

"And I am invited to sup with him in his private rooms at six of the clock this evening."

She toasted me with her tea dish. "And the prospect is still agreeable to you?"

Having reached the crux of the matter concerning me, I nodded then confided, "I cannot deny it, but my ambition is, as it ever was, to protect George, and I would leif not discomfort him by producing a younger sibling who would take precedence over him for the fact of who sired it. I have been married and birthed a child, but given my age when I married my husband, I am unworldly. I would forgo the honour of bearing a royal bastard if you have any knowledge you would share with me?"

She set down her tea dish and nodded. "In lieu of your mother passing before you were old enough for the secret to be shared, I gift to you this advice…" She made a ring of her finger and thumb. "Require your maid to cut a disc of sea-sponge thus big and soak it with vinegar or the juice of a lemon, then push it into your womanly opening as high as it will go. It will be as soft as your inner place should be. Your lover will not feel the presence of it. Do not remove it before it has had time to render his seed harmless—no less than half a dozen hours after the completion of your love-making."

I smiled my relief. "I thank you, Your Grace."

She looked at the timepiece on the mantel. "But you should run away. 'Tis nearly four, and you need time to array yourself in your finery if the king is expecting you at Whitehall by six."

I kissed her cheek then walked up the stairs to Hannah, a picture forming in my mind of how I wished to appear before His Majesty while I climbed them.

Hannah dipped her curtsey as I entered my rooms. "The first of thy new gowns has arrived should you wish to wear it this evening?"

I shook my head. "I shall dress in my male attire tonight, and when you fetch my washing water, bring with it a glass containing fresh lemon juice, please."

She left me, returned with the item I'd requested twenty minutes later, and offered me the glass with pursed lips as if imagining the sourness of its contents. "You did not say whether it should be sweetened, my lady, so I have not done so. Shall I return to the kitchen and make it more palatable?"

"No. It is not for drinking but for a matter more personal. I am invited to sup in private with King Charles this evening, and the duchess advises that with an application of lemon I may escape the consequences of doing so."

She spluttered. "The king? *In private!* Oh, my lady, assuredly you must wear your finest gown?"

I smiled. "Assuredly I must not, for our Sovereign finds my person dressed as a lad an appealing prospect."

She looked doubtful but took the tray into the dressing room without further comment, set it down, and selected the outfit I'd requested.

I walked through the doorway. "Dispense with the shirt and ruffled jabot, if you please. The waistcoat will suffice."

Her eyes widened. "But, my lady, the ensemble is barely decent with it, without…."

I turned my back for her to unfasten my gown. "I will wear the unremarkable black cloak my husband gave me and keep it close around me outside of the king's rooms. Now, let us get on. I am bidden to be at Whitehall by six."

She prepared my washing water with scent and wine then removed my clothes, cleansed, dried, and talc'd my body, and I nodded at the sea-sponge when she finished while forming a circle with my fingers.

"Cut me a piece this size from it, if you would."

She fetched the scissors from her work basket and did so, then I took it and the glass of lemon to my personal closet and did as my godmother had advised.

Hannah dressed me on my return. I refused my stockings as well as my shirt and asked for satin dance pumps rather than leather shoes, then she refreshed my ringlets and cosmetics. I turned this way and that in front of the mirror when she was done, admired the tight fit of my breeches along with the amount of bare flesh and cleavage I had on show, moistened my lips, and winked at my reflection.

"So, let us discover whether a female dressed as I am has ever come your way, Your Majesty."

Hannah snorted. "I expect not."

I smiled. "As do I."

Hannah placed my cloak over my shoulders, and I clutched it around me.

"I am due to arrive at the palace by way of the water but do not care to return home in the same manner after dark. Instruct Silas to bring my coach to Whitehall and await my joining him at the Holbein Gate once the sun sets."

"He will be there, my lady."

I nodded, left my rooms, and raised my hood as I left the house to avoid any undue speculation as to where I maybe going should I encounter anyone I knew en route. Only one barge awaited the prospect of a fare, its wherryman wearing a waistcoat of purple, and he nodded as if expecting me.

I stepped onto the barge, and he punted us down the river. I alighted at a jetty and recognised the king's highest-ranked servant, William Chiffinch, Keeper of the King's Private

Closet, standing upon it. He beckoned, and I knew from the manner of his addressing me the king had not informed him of the identity of his guest.

"Come hither, my pretty."

I followed, and he confided over his shoulder, "Our Sovereign is a lusty man, and you are privileged to have caught his royal eye. Be assured if you perform to his pleasure, I will escort thee down afterwards, and you will depart with suitable reward."

I smiled beneath the privacy of my hood and didn't resist amusing myself a little at his expense. "Such as?"

He chuckled. "Never you fear, my pretty. We shall find you a little trinket or two."

I pictured my diamonds and forbore to tease him further over his mistaking the utilitarian nature of the drab cloak I wore. "I thank you, sir, but that will not be necessary."

He nodded then led the way along several, draughty corridors until at last I recognised the stairs that led to Mistress Palmer's rooms. He did not climb them but guided me down an adjacent hallway with a door at its far end, the royal feathers carved in high relief upon it.

He tapped and bowed me in. "Your guest, Sire."

I entered the room. King Charles sat before his fire clad in an ankle-length silk dressing gown, richly embroidered, his feet tucked into matching slippers. He waved his dismissal at Chiffinch, and when the door closed, looked at me.

"I give thee a good evening, Lady Emma, if indeed 'tis you beneath the hood?"

I lifted it down and tried for an air of assurance, though I felt as nervously skittish as a foal. "If I am the lady you are expecting, then yes, it is I."

His lips tilted into a smile. "No other would be welcome at this time. Will you not step closer?"

I looked into his eyes, and my hands shook to the flutter in my belly. I unfastened my cloak and let it fall to floor. "Or mayhap my naughty brother would be your preference?"

He gazed at my barely clothed body, and his irises darkened. "Come and stand before me." His voice, soft and low, his words were a seductive request not an order.

I complied to ripples of excited expectation running through my thighs.

"Disrobe?"

I unbuttoned my waistcoat, parted it to display the roundness of my breasts, then shrugged it off to his murmur.

"Mmmm…definitely not a boy, but very naughty all the same."

I toed off my pumps, released the buttons of my breeches, wriggled them down and off, and his cock hardened beneath his dressing gown as he gazed at the muff between my legs.

"So, truly flaxen-haired. Turn?"

I pirouetted, my mound wet, my nipples hard, a feeling of utter wantonness coming over me at the intensity of his stare and the erection tenting the front of his robe.

His voice deepened to a throaty growl. "Kneel?"

I did so. He parted his dressing gown, and my breath caught at my first sight of an erect male cock that to my certainty was a deal larger than the one that had penetrated me before, even though I'd never been permitted to view it.

He rasped, "Explore my boy and the bags beneath him. Taste. Use your mouth."

I needed no second urging and stroked his smooth length, licking the flavour of him onto my tongue as I fastened my mouth over his prick, my fingers seeking the shape of the hairy orbs beneath it. I sucked as I would on a spear of buttered asparagus until he emitted a low groan.

"Ride me."

I stood, straddled his lap, eased his cockhead through my wetness, and whimpered when I sank down on his length. He claimed my mouth with his and cupped my breasts, circling his thumbs over and around my hard nipples. I sighed my pleasure, swayed my hips to feel him deeper inside me, and he grasped my buttocks.

"Bounce. Take your fill."

I did so and squeaked when his shaft rubbed on the sensitive spot inside me. "Oh…oh…oh!" I moved faster and faster, grinding down to the urging of his hands until muscles contracted in my groin, then spread, to his deeply groaned, "Yes… We are there. Your peach is as sweet and tight as my boy likes it…"

I moaned. Waves of pleasure ran through my belly and thighs, and we stilled, breathing hard— until the king's stomach emitted a mighty grumble. I giggled.

He lifted my chin with his fingers and kissed my lips. "Od's fish! You are indeed a naughty lad. Supper was supposed to come afore this."

With only one sponge finger since I broke my fast to fill my belly, the thought of food caused my middle to growl near as loud as his had. I disengaged from his cock. He chuckled, put his hand into his pocket, and offered me a linen

125

handkerchief. I wiped and reached for my clothes. He stood, poured wine from a flagon into two glasses, and gave one to me.

I accepted it and sipped.

He took my other hand and led me to a table, laid with place settings for two, and an array of covered dishes set upon it. "Would you mind to serve, or I could call Chiffinch to do so?"

I shook my head. "No. I am not so precious that to spoon supper onto our plates is beneath my talent."

He sat. "As warms my heart, for indeed, I am a hungry fellow and oft kept waiting for my food while correct protocol is followed."

I thought of what I'd read of his vigorous exercise regime—a swim in the Thames every morn at dawn while his retinue waited shivering on the banks cursing the coolness of daybreak, followed by an hour of tennis before beginning his royal duties, then looked at his lean, long-limbed figure and chided him as I lifted the first cover.

"I am neither your wife nor your mother, but I have been both. You must demand your vittles with more urgency, given the activity and length of your day."

He chuckled. "You look like neither of those, my naughty lad, but your words strike a chord with me, and I shall endeavour to do so."

I investigated the supper on offer. A juicy duck roasted with plums, succulent pig cheeks in a rich wine sauce, yellow cheese, griddled onion, and fine white bread. I placed a generous portion of each onto his plate, set it before him, then took a serving for myself and sat.

He speared his duck and cut into it. "So, no longer a wife but still a mother. How fares it for you without a husband to oversee your interests?"

Though I knew of his fondness for family matters and children, his broaching the subject without me having to think of a way to introduce it relieved my mind. I sliced into a piece of pork on my plate and sighed. "It would go better for me if I could think of a solution to prevent those who would steal my son's inheritance from him."

He frowned. "Who seeks to?"

I added some onion to my fork with a louder sigh. "My Uncle John, for one. He hounds me to sign George's revenue over to him. I wish I had a higher authority I could appeal to."

His nose wrinkled with distaste. "I have no fondness for the Duke of Portchester. He did not aid my father by sending us armed men to fight our war, but only sent a bag or two of coins in support of our cause."

I offered my loaded fork to the king's lips. "You hold me surprised he even offered that much."

He accepted my mouthful. "So, have you any thoughts on what could be done to thwart him?"

I nibbled on a piece of cheese, my heart pounding as I came to the crux of the matter. "Mayhap, if someone higher ranked in the natural order than my uncle were to write me a letter expressing their interest in George's well-being and acknowledge that in the unavoidable absence of the father, a mother will always be the next best fiercest protector of her child's future funds, he would desist with his efforts to coerce me into signing my son's inheritance into his wardship?"

He tore a piece of bread and dipped it in his gravy. "I believe I agree with that sentiment. Of a certainty, my mother has always been my staunchest supporter. Every penny she could raise during our exile she gave into my hands while she herself begged on the charity of her family. Your predicament gives me cause for concern. I myself shall write to you in the manner you have suggested."

I smiled my happiness and scooped up a mouthful of succulent duck covered in plum sauce. "I thank you for your generosity, Sire. You relieve my mind. I have a young cousin in my care, Miss Bonnitta DeVere. If you would include her in your good wishes?"

He smiled. "Of course. 'Tis little enough you ask of me compared to some others."

I chewed my meat and let the matter drop so as not to bore him on the subject and instead asked his opinion of the current fashion at the French Court and advice on the care required for tiny curly-eared puppies until he laid down his knife and fork. I glanced at the clock on the mantel and couldn't believe how quickly time had flown while I had chattered on, easy in his company, and I silently apologised to his queen.

"I believe your royal duty awaits, as does my escort home. If you would excuse me, Sire?"

His eyes followed mine to the clock, then he gazed at the roundness of my breasts rising from the 'V' of my waistcoat. "Your understanding delights me, though if it was down to the preference of my boy…"

I stood with a smile. "My evening in your company has been an honour and a pleasure. If you would request your servant to show me out?"

He called his name then draped my cloak around my shoulders with a soft kiss on the top of my head. "The pleasure and honour were mine."

Chiffinch entered the room and bowed. "I will escort you to the wherry if you would care to accompany me?"

I curtsied my farewell to King Charles and followed his servant from the room. He surveyed my uncovered head with an awareness in his eyes that his previous honorific of 'my pretty' had been inappropriate as he closed the door behind us.

"I believe I misjudged the plainness of your attire earlier. My apology, my lady."

I smiled my understanding. "I thank you, but they are unnecessary. I expect some guests feel overwhelmed to be here, and I'm sure your familiar manner in addressing them is of comfort. If you hold a jewel or coins in your pocket, gift them to the next working girl who arrives here, excited to be so, but trembling in her shoes?"

He nodded. "Willingly. Is there any different service I could render you?"

"Only that I would like to leave Whitehall street-side rather than by way the wherry pier. My coach and servant await me there."

"Of course, my lady."

He escorted me along the hallway, now lit in the dark of late evening by thick, slow-burn candles set into wall sconces and towards the foot of the stairs that led to Mistress Palmer's apartment—but before we reached them, her voice, shrill and furious, rang out.

"I tell you I will not stand for it! How dare he? I will have him beg my forgiveness for this."

Then the Duke of Buckingham's voice. "Calm yourself, Barbara. Your bad temper is not attractive and quite frankly two-faced. You take other lovers when it suits, as does he. Od's blood! Your bed is still warm from our love-making earlier this evening."

"Irrelevant! I will not take second place to some drab nobody Chiffinch has picked up for him from Jesu knows where!"

The shadows cast by the flickering light told me I had no choice but to meet her, so I squared my shoulders and prepared to face her wrath.

She caught sight of me as she turned into the hallway and she punched Buckingham's upper arm. "What did I tell you! I knew it!"

I walked closer to the sconce nearest them, illuminating my face. "Your Grace. Mistress Palmer. I give you good evening."

Buckingham laughed. "Hoisted by your own petard, Barbara. 'Tis not a nobody but Countess Summerly."

Her breath hissed through her teeth. "Whatever your title, I will be first with him even should your visit here tonight result in your bearing his child, for I have birthed one to him ahead of you!"

I stared her down. "Then know me better and believe that outcome is in no way desirable on my part. I have been honoured by the king's attention. If that results in his writing a letter expressing his interest in the welfare of my son and cousin, I will hold myself satisfied."

Her eyes reflected her confusion as my words sank in. "You wish for a letter? That is all?"

I nodded and gave her a parting shot by opening my cloak to give her sight of the scant clothing I wore beneath it. "Yes, only that—but still the burden of state affairs the king carries is a worry to me. Mayhap those more often in his company might like to have a care not to let the matter slip from his mind lest I have to return and refresh his memory for myself."

Buckingham's gaze raked my body to his grin. "Barbara, I believe you have been outdone."

I closed my cloak and swept past them with a final warning, not caring whether Chiffinch followed in my wake. "I give you three days."

He caught up with me as I turned in the direction the king and Mistress Palmer had taken when leaving the palace to go to the park. "If you please, Lady Emma, allow me continue to escort you out? Our Sovereign will be unhappy if I cannot tell him I have seen you safely on your way."

I nodded and slowed my steps to accompany him through the twisting labyrinth that comprised the palace of Whitehall.

He bowed when we reached the Holbein Gate. "I bid thee farewell, and much as I shouldn't say it, it gladdened my heart to see that particular lady given a dose of her own medicine. You will receive your letter. I promise it."

I raised my hood. "I thank you, sir. I was truly honoured to be granted a little private time with His Majesty. I will never forget it, nor his understanding of my need to protect my child. I bid thee good evening."

Silas held a flambeau aloft to illuminate the crest on the door of my carriage. I climbed in and spent the journey home revisiting the pleasure I had experienced at the hands of a lover who desired me as I did him.

Chapter Seven

Hannah undressed me on my return home, but my night's slumber did not prove restful, and I woke in the morning to snatches of half-remembered dreams, my body trembling with desire, not for the man who had introduced me to the pleasure of love-making, but for a certain green-eyed someone who had done no more than kiss my hand. My skin felt hot, my face flushed, and I silently admonished myself. *This will not do! George and Bonnie are in no way safe as yet.*

I sat up, rearranged the pillows at my back, and the bedroom door opened. Hannah stepped in, laid my tray across my thighs, and Franny strolled into the room behind her. He perched on the side of bed, dismissed her with a wave of his hand, and smiled.

"So, dearest heart. Mama told me where you ate your supper last evening. Lay it all before me, I beg? Does his cannon, indeed, fire as mightily as legend tells it so?"

I near split the hot cocoa off my tray onto the bed and snorted. "Franny!"

His eyes sparkling into mine, he smirked. "Did you not expect me to ask? 'Tis, after all, a subject of interest to me. I will never so much as glimpse his magnificent weapon first-hand, for sadly, his taste runs only to female company, so your account will have to suffice to satisfy my curiosity."

I giggled and recalled my evening as I broke a piece off my cinnamon roll. "My apologies for failing to take a measuring stick with me, but if I were to hazard a guess, I would say mayhap three inches short of a foot with the girth of a thick, well-grown winter carrot."

His smirk widened into a full-mouthed grin. "A carrot! You have just likened His Majesty's love digit to a carrot?"

I sniggered. "Well, it wasn't orange, nor tapered at its end, but you take my meaning?"

He laughed. "I do, my sweet, though I'm not sure I will ever be able to look at our beloved Sovereign again without picturing that particular vegetable, nor eat one without him coming to mind."

I laughed with him then straightened my face. "I also managed to make an enemy of Mistress Palmer last evening. I came across her as I left the king. She must have received word he was entertaining another and was on her way to confront him."

Franny frowned. "Why he allows her to berate him when in a high temper is a mystery to many, and her imperious ways do not endear her to those who live and serve within the palace. If you were seen by a page or a lackey in Chiffinch's company, word would have been whispered in her ear, even if just out of spite. Did you accomplish that which you set out to do and receive his promise?"

I nodded.

"Then do not let her ill-will trouble you, my sweet. For what harm can she cause you now?"

I considered the matter, and in particular, the sustained effort required by those vying for the king's good graces to satisfy their ambitions and extract gifts of titles and wealth from him. "I have not the appetite to become further entangled in the web of court intrigue surrounding the king. A high title, ample income, and jewels are already mine. So long as I receive my letter, I have no need to whore myself further, and if I am no longer competing with Mistress Palmer for his favour, she will turn her attention to others who are, I should think."

Franny's eyes widened, and he spluttered, "My angel, you are no whore! Do not think it!"

I squared my shoulders and lifted my chin. "Whether for a letter only of value to me or a collar of jewels worth a small fortune, I did not bed him solely for pleasure. I have joined the ranks of the king's whores, I will not deny it, but it was an honest trade of favours, and I will feel no shame for having done so."

He growled. "I should think not. It was little enough you asked of him."

I relaxed against my pillows. "You echo his words to me. He was kindness itself and his company a pleasure. He would be an easy man to love, I believe, if not for his weakness to discover the delights beneath the skirt of every pretty female that catches his eye."

Franny smiled. "You will receive your letter, methinks. Many seek the king's promise, but he does not give it lightly."

I nodded. "Chiffinch expressed his contentment that I gave back to Mistress Palmer twice as much as she did me and assured me I would."

He chuckled. "Then you will. Chiffinch has been on the receiving end of Palmer's more violent tantrums and hit by the objects she throws during them as to give him no fondness for her, and his influence with His Majesty is immense."

The sparkle returned to his eyes as I laughed with him, and he revealed the cause of it when he said, "Last evening, I myself attended a select soiree at the White Swan Inn, where the Beefsteak Club had gathered to partake of dinner, but before I could, Rochester and I discovered a mutual urge to sup together without other company."

I smiled. "I am glad for you, my Adonis, but what of Edgeware?"

He wrinkled his nose. "He has some odd notions at times. I will make it clear we are no

139

longer intimate friends the next time we meet, but for now, would you care to accompany me to Rochester House and listen to the poets invited there to recite their latest works?"

I broke a piece off my roll and dipped it into my fast-cooling cocoa. "I would be delighted to, I thank you."

Franny stood and blew me a kiss. "Then it shall be so, my angel. I will await the glory of your presence in the library."

The door closed behind him.

I ate my breakfast with haste before it became any more unpalatable, put my feet to the floor, and used my closet to remove the sea sponge, then called Hannah's name. She walked into my bedroom carrying a pitcher of steaming water.

"My new gown, show it to me, if you would?"

She set down the water, brought it to me, and I smiled at the sight of it—silver and gold thread woven into a flowered brocade.

"'Tis lovely. I will wear it for my outing with Lord Francombe."

I followed her to the dressing room and, once washed and powdered, stepped into my petticoat and dress. I looked into the mirror as she fastened it and was delighted with the touches of London finesse—the bodice fitting so perfectly it emphasised the smallness my waist, the neckline more daring than on the gowns Hannah had altered for me, and a shorter skirt-length to show a glimpse of my ankle.

I sat. Hannah applied my cosmetics, curled my hair, and added gold ribbons to clusters of curls she gathered on each side of my head. I selected a large sapphire drop suspended on a gold chain that sat between the rising moons of my breasts and spotted my coin pouch on the side table.

I nodded towards it. "Take a shilling with one of my ribbons of either burgundy or blue and require a page to run to the royal kennels. They are to provide recompense for the kennel lad, Will the younger. He donated the one tying his hair to provide collars for my pups."

She bobbed, and I walked down the stairs to find Franny.

He smiled when I entered the library. "As ever, you are ravishing, my love. Let us away. Our carriage awaits."

I took his arm. "Does Rochester not find it inconvenient to be without direct access to the river?"

He nodded. "Very. He is looking at three possible sites on which to build a new London home, though each is a little farther from Whitehall than is ideal, hence his hesitation."

I stepped into the carriage and sat. "The Summerly Estate possesses a town house not so far from your own. It is disgracefully damp, built only of wattle and daub, which is why I preferred not to stay there for my visit, but it stands on a generous grant of land."

He took his place beside me. "You would sell such an asset to him?"

"Of a certainty, I would be prepared to seek Mr FitzWilliam's advice on the subject. George has no need for a London residence for several years yet, and by the time he does, considerations other than access to the river may have come into play. I received word yesterday. Mr FitzWilliam will be attending the capital on estate business in the next sennight or so."

Franny smiled. "I am sure Rochester would jump at such an opportunity. Describe to me your Mr FitzWilliam that I might recognise him should I come across him in Town when not in your company."

Nothing loathe, I brought Hugo to mind. "He is tall, not so high as King Charles, but several inches more than most men. Broader across the shoulders than His Majesty, his hair is as black and fashionably curled, but he has no moustache, and his eyes are green. He wears a gold signet on his right hand engraved with his family crest of crossed swords and a lion rampant."

Franny's eyebrows rose to my description of Hugo's appearance and insignia. "From a bastard royal line, then?"

"With Fitz as part of his name, I would presume it, but I've never enquired."

The carriage pulled up, and a footman directed us to the Long Gallery where we found many persons gathered, although Rochester appeared at Franny's side before we had taken two steps inside the room. He clicked his fingers at a lackey, and we took a glass of wine apiece from the offered tray.

"Lady Emma, you are welcome. Your appearance is divine. Francombe, your company last evening was a delight. Shall we sup together again tonight?"

Franny glanced at me. "We will if my angel has no plans for me and would excuse my doing so?"

I smiled. "I am more than happy to attend the duchess. Her dinners are delicious, and the card games afterwards are fun."

They met each other's eyes for a moment then offered me an arm each, and we moved through the room until I spied Lord Saltash and Lady Helen.

Saltash bowed. "Golden goddess before whom...."

Lady Helen interrupted him with a snort. "Salty, no!"

I laughed. "Three times in three days, my lord. Really?"

He smiled his satisfaction at his smoking of me. "Well, you never know. Repeated oft enough, you may come to appreciate the smoothness of my phrasing."

Lord Exeter joined us. "I have secured chairs for the ladies, if you would care to sit?"

We followed him and did so. The males ranged themselves behind us, Franny and Rochester aligned as to leave no gap between their shoulders and arms, then we listened to the odes on offer, though some of them were so long-winded I opened my fan and used it to cover my yawn.

An interval was announced, to my relief, and I excused myself to visit the ladies' withdrawing room. With no actual need to use the potty chair, I lingered before the mirror and tweaked my hair while acknowledging I did not possess the soul of a poet and hoping that when the recitals resumed, they would be briefer than they had been before.

I delayed leaving the room until the moment it would have been rude to dally longer and heard but one voice droning on when I opened the door. I stepped outside, intent on returning to my seat in the Long Gallery as silently as I had left the one in Franny's box during the interval at the theatre, and gasped as a hand was placed over my mouth. Stronger arms than mine manhandled me back inside and pressed me against the door, preventing it from being reopened.

"So, I have lost my lover and 'twill be by your doing. I know it!"

At the sound of his hateful voice, I sank my teeth into the soft flesh of Edgeware's palm, and with a sharp intake of breath, he snatched it away, though his confining of me did not lessen.

"So, still you challenge me, madam? You should behave with more compliance towards your future husband's comfort, lest you reap the rewards for not doing so when we are wed."

My bile rose, along with my temper. I stamped down hard on the tender spot of his foot unprotected by the leather of his shoe, then kicked out so the sharp edge of the heel of mine caught his shin. He swore and released his hold on me.

I twisted away from him and spat, "Understand this, my lord. We are *not* going to be wed!"

His eyes watered in pain, but his mouth twisted into a cold smile. "We shall see, madam. We shall see."

I wrenched the door open and could not help but notice his hardened cock pressing against the front of his breeches when I walked away. I beckoned a lackey, requested he convey my apologies to Franny for my having to depart the recital due to the onset of a headache, and had his coachman drive me home before returning to Rochester House to await his master.

I contemplated going in search of my godmother's advice as to Edgeware's behaviour but decided to hold my peace until I had spoken to Franny on the subject and instead made my way to my rooms to recover my composure by imbibing a large glass of wine. A lively dinner and card evening soothed my discomfort a little more, and my fears receded further when a letter bearing the royal seal was delivered to my rooms the following morning after Hannah had dressed me in my gold gown ruched up on one side to display my silver petticoat.

I opened it, and my hand trembled with excitement when his words expressed every sentiment I'd hoped for in the warmest terms, the handwriting the king's own, not that of another to which he'd appended his signature. A newfound security lightened my mood, and I reread his words until I could not keep still any longer and jumped up to dance around the room. Franny opened the door, and I held my letter out to him.

"It is here. Read it, if you will? It is perfect."

He took it from me and cast his eyes down the page. "He gives you leave to bring any matter of concern to his attention. Excellent! And states his belief a mother is the fittest guardian of her child's interests. Even better!"

My smile widened as I twirled around. "And he includes Bonnie."

He nodded. "So he does. *'Our trust in yourself extends to near relations in your care, such as Miss DeVere…'* Has this helped to amend your headache, my angel? Did you feel unwell due to the anxiety of waiting to know whether you would receive it?"

I stilled my giddy dance in the face of his concern. "No… Not that." I walked to the consul table, poured two glasses of wine, perched on the sofa, and looked expectantly at the space beside me.

Franny sat, and I handed him a glass.

"I excused myself due to the discomfort I felt at the manner in which Edgeware behaved towards me during the interval between the readings. You remarked he had some odd notions. Will you share them with me?"

He frowned and sat straighter. "I dislike the sound of that. Tell me, if you please, what occurred?"

I sipped. "Despite my protests to the contrary, he seems to believe our marriage is of such a surety he has the command of a husband over my person. I resisted his demands, but my doing so resulted in his cock becoming aroused."

Franny swore. "The devil take him! Forgive me, my sweet. Though I knew Edgeware's taste ran to females as well as males, it was not a subject of interest to me, so I did not enquire too closely."

"Of course you did not. Why would you?"

"Until you arrived, I had no motive to do so, but my affection for you has caused me to take more note of his utterances. Edgeware is considerate towards men, but I do not believe he holds females in the same esteem. A woman's place is to obey and conform to a man's wishes."

I admitted my confusion. "But my resistance aroused him even though I kicked him hard enough to bring tears to his eyes?"

Franny squeezed my hand. "I cannot swear to it, but I suspect his pleasure was not caused by the pain, but rather by thoughts of his subduing you when you finally concede to your uncle's instruction and accept your fate."

I swallowed a mouthful of my wine. "I suspected as much. I will take care not to give him the opportunity to find me alone again."

"You should not be put to such lengths."

I returned the pressure of his hand. "'Tis the lot of a solitary female, but should rumour of the king's interest in me circulate, he will desist, I think."

He nodded. "Then be assured…word will fly on wings. Would you care to attend Lady Berry's musical entertainment with me this evening so I may begin to send it on its way?"

I smiled. "That would be delightful, my Adonis."

He set down his glass and kissed my hand. "I will meet you in the Tapestry room to partake of supper, then we can leave Mama to her cards and make our way to our own party by water."

I folded my precious letter into its original creases when the door closed behind him, secured it within the jewel chest containing my mother's diamonds, then sat at the desk to pen a few words to Bonnie. I imagined her happiness at receiving them being akin to mine own and smiled as my nib scratched across the vellum. I appended the '*E*' of my chosen moniker, and a tap sounded on the door. I bid my caller enter, expecting a servant with a message, but it was Lady Helen who walked into the room.

She frowned her concern into my eyes. "I find you recovered and in good health this day, I hope?"

I smiled. "You do, I thank you. A minor inconvenience necessitated my early departure from the recital, but I am quite well now."

She closed the door and moved closer. "Would that inconvenience, mayhap, have been in the shape of Lord Francombe's ill-natured friend who I saw follow you from the room and return to it bearing a slight limp he did not previously possess?"

I shrugged, not wishing to tell an untruth nor become the possible subject of unsavoury innuendo for admitting the particulars of the matter. "Possibly…but 'twas a small misadventure I do not dwell on."

She sat on the chair nearest the desk with a sigh. "Should you confide in me, I promise your words will go no further. Indeed, I wish you would, for given Edgeware's title and wealth, Salty hints I should make myself agreeable and encourage his attentions."

I saw only honest enquiry in her eyes, so advised, "I should not do so if I were you. Lord Francombe knows his thinking better than most and believes he does not hold females in high regard, as has been my experience on the few occasions I have met him socially. Forgive me...but, I presume, given the nobility of your birth, you have a healthy dowry and no need to seek him as a suitor?"

She blushed. "No. Other than I value my brother's opinion above all things and would accept his preference should I have no strong feeling against his choice."

I smiled. "Do not hold Lord Saltash at fault. Franny tells me Edgeware is a man of charm when in the company of other men. 'Tis only when alone with a female his true nature shows."

Her colour deepened as the words burst from her lips. "'Tis Exeter I want for mine husband, but he and Salty have been close friends since boyhood, and I cannot get him to view me as anything other than a younger sister."

I considered the neckline of her dress, scooped but virginally high, and thought that though her bosom and waist were larger than mine, we were not that dissimilar in figure that I could not lend her a dress if it was fastened at the front with ribbons rather than pins or buttons at the back. "Mayhap we should try and change that perspective with a more womanly gown?"

She smiled. "Oh, I would like that exceedingly. Mama grows increasingly vague with each passing year and believes I am still fifteen rather than one and twenty when the dressmaker calls."

I smiled and called Hannah's name. She entered the room and bobbed. "My lady?"

I considered Helen's brunette hair and hazel eyes. "The green dress you amended for me, bring it here, if you would?"

She did so, and Helen sighed. "'Tis beautiful…"

I nodded at Hannah. "Lady Helen desires a change of gown, with mayhap a rearrangement of her hair and a little more blush to her lips?"

Hannah curtsied, and Helen followed her out. I folded my letter to Bonnie, heated wax to seal it, and excitement bubbled from her when the door opened not too many minutes later.

"Your maid is a wonder! Exeter will not be able to mistake the matter now!"

I looked at her lips, full and pink, her womanly assets now highlighted by my gown, and smiled. "Would you care to hazard a guess as to where he might be found this fine day?"

She laughed. "Salty escorted me here then departed to seek Exeter that they may walk to St James' park and view the royal hunt."

I offered her my hand. "Shall we follow and discover whether they are still about their business?"

She clasped it. "'Oh, yes. 'Tis a fine day for an airing, I believe."

We smirked at each other and left the house. The sun's heat had dimmed, but without a breeze to stir the air, I did not feel the lack of a shawl or cloak while we strolled along, nodding to the acquaintances we met along the way. The park came in sight, and a buzz stirred at the sound of hooves on cobbles. People turned, including me, towards the scarlet-and-gold quartered livery of the riders, three in front and three behind the dark-haired man mounted on a pure-bred stallion in their midst. I gazed at Hugo, willing him to notice me, but concentrating on his task, he did not.

The lady behind me sighed. "Is that one of Baron FitzWilliam's sons?"

Her companion sighed louder. "I believe it is. I wonder whose livery escorts him?"

Lady Helen nudged my arm. "Well, well. A handsome man newly arrived in Town. That'll cause a stir. More so if he is the elder son. I do not recognise the livery, though. Do you?"

I answered airily to disguise the fact my heart was doing some very strange things inside my chest. "Oh, 'tis my livery. Mr FitzWilliam has come to Town to execute some business on behalf of the Summerly Estate, and he is not the baron's heir but his younger son."

"Shame, but still, I predict he will be much in demand."

I didn't hiss at the thought, though it was a close-run thing.

We entered the park, its outer edges cultivated and laid with gravel paths for those on foot—the remainder, a natural wilderness and the habitat of the prey King Charles hunted for his table. Several male heads turned towards us as we walked, and I noticed a trend. The eyes of those Helen didn't acknowledge gleamed in appreciation, and those of the men she knew and greeted seemed to widen slightly in surprise.

She pinched the back of my hand. "There they are, up ahead."

Lord Exeter's gaze did not leave her when we approached. Exeter offered Lady Helen his arm. I accepted Lord Saltash's, and we ambled along behind them.

"She wishes him for her husband, you know?"

He frowned. "I did not see it before today, though mayhap I should have. My sister has not been short of offers and refused them all. Exeter has received every encouragement to pursue at least three heiresses, none of them ill-favoured, and has not done so."

I glanced at him. "So, will you encourage the match?"

"There can be no objection to their marrying should they desire it."

I smiled. "Then I foresee your closest friend will become your brother-in-law before too much longer."

The worry lines disappeared from his forehead, and he smiled. "I would like that. Helen will be a wonderful wife and married to a man I know will treat her with respect."

I agreed. "A most happy outcome given the lottery that is marriage."

He stopped by a bench seat. "May we pause a while?"

I sat.

He did the same, then asked, "How did you fare in the previous lottery? Was your union happy?"

I answered him honestly, as he deserved for the attention he had paid to me since we had first met. "Not especially. My late husband was a joyless man of dour disposition…but it gifted me my son, George, whom I adore."

He gazed into my eyes. "And would you like more children to love? For George to enjoy the rough and tumble of family life?"

I guessed what he was really asking me and let him down as gently as I could. "I may, but the interests of the child I've already born will always come first with me. I would not discomfort George by bearing a younger sibling, that if male, would take precedence over him for the fact of its father being of higher rank than his own."

He sighed. "You would not care to be a duchess?"

I leaned towards him and kissed his cheek. "I'm sure we would deal together perfectly well, but I thank you, no. You deserve a wife devoted to your interests alone, without obligation to another."

His cheeks flushed at the touch of my lips. "Well, I would have liked it exceedingly, but I honour you for your loyalty to your son."

I stood and called a halt to the subject. "Then let us resume our walk with no awkwardness between us. You shall be as extravagant in your compliments to me as you have been before, and I shall continue to laugh at you for your smoking of me when you do."

He rose and offered me his arm. "You really are the most comfortable female to be around, apart from my sister."

I placed my hand on his forearm and smiled. "Comfortable, my lord? Are you quite sure a *golden goddess who puts the midday orb to shame* can be described thus?"

He laughed. "See, I knew you would come to appreciate my phrasing."

We strolled on, chatting with the ease of friends, and caught up with Exeter and Lady Helen standing side by side admiring the swans on the lake.

Lord Saltash opened the case of his silver pocket watch. "Lady Berry's soiree begins in less than two hours. If you ladies require a change of dress for the event, we should direct our footsteps home."

Lady Helen glanced down at her borrowed gown, then at me with a plea in her eyes.

I answered her unspoken question to spare her from having to ask it out loud in front of Lord Exeter. "Lady Helen, would you care to return to my rooms with me? My maid would be happy to refresh our appearance, I'm sure."

She smiled her acceptance, so we linked our arms and walked to the Melville residence with the gentlemen following along behind us. They left us at the portico, and I led the way up the stairs. She twirled so my gown swayed around her legs and laughed her delight when I shut the door to my sitting room behind us.

"I believe it worked. He could barely take his eyes from me. I thank you for allowing me to continue wearing your dress this evening."

I shook my head. "There is no chance you will be attending Lady Berry's soiree dressed in the same gown he saw you in this afternoon when I have a rose-pink that will suit you just as well."

Her smile lit her eyes. "You would lend me another?"

"No. I am gifting them to you if they will not put you in your mother's bad graces should she catch sight of you wearing a gown of lower décolletage than she approves of."

She hugged me. "I shall add a muslin neckerchief when I'm at home and feel no shame for removing it as I leave the house. I am one and twenty and should be permitted to dress like a woman, not a girl."

I squeezed her back and called Hannah's name.

She entered by way of the door that connected it to my bedroom. "My lady?"

"Lady Helen has joined me so we may make ourselves ready to attend this evening's entertainment together. Lay out my new gown of brocade and the one rose-pink, please."

She bobbed and offered me a folded note. "Mr FitzWilliam called this afternoon."

My heart thumped as I took it and read.

With regret, I find you not at home. H.F.

A wave of disappointment ran through me, but I didn't let it show on my face as I dismissed Hannah to lay out the gowns I had requested. I poured two glasses of wine, handed one to Lady Helen, and tried not to appear abstracted while we re-dressed in our evening attire.

Hannah handed me my fan as the clock struck seven, and I walked with Lady Helen to the Tapestry room.

Chapter Eight

Franny stood waiting as he had promised he would be and bowed to us. "My delight in the evening is assured. I shall be the envy of all when I arrive at the soiree accompanied by two females of utter perfection, one on each arm."

We curtsied our appreciation of his compliment, and after dinner he escorted us to the wherry pier. The boatman punted us down the river, and Franny led us inside to a ballroom lit with a myriad of candles. Exeter and Saltash hovered just inside its doors, and if Exeter's expression was anything to go by, he appreciated the sight of Lady Helen wearing my rose-coloured gown as much as he had the green.

Conversation hummed around the room. Lord Saltash greeted me and kissed my hand. I smiled and looked beyond him, my eyes drawn to the corner of the room where the buzz was loudest—and saw Hugo, standing in the midst of an animated group. My heart double-tapped, and though I couldn't hear his words, I watched his lips move. His mannerisms were so familiar to me, I smiled, my body feeling as if it had softened and melted—and it struck me with a force that near took my breath away. I didn't just desire Hugo. I loved him. The sensation raced through me, and I turned away, not wishing to be caught staring.

More guests entered the ballroom, and the excited hum increased at the sight of the king with Mistress Palmer on his arm, his retinue of close friends following on behind them. She acknowledged my presence with a small smile, and I returned the same compliment to herself.

Franny noted our exchange and leaned close. "You have made your peace?"

I murmured into his ear. "I did inform her of the extent of my ambition, so if she's aware King

Charles has written to me she will also know I pose no further threat to her dominance of him."

He nodded. "She'll have a servant or two in her pay to inform her of his business. Glance over my shoulder and tell me his reaction?"

I did so, and my already tumultuous heartbeat raced faster when all other eyes in the room seemed to swivel towards me. "I believe the king is leading her this way."

Franny pinched the back of my hand with a soft, triumphant hiss. "Yesss. Well done, my angel. Most of the queen's current difficulties are due to her refusal to acknowledge Palmer as his maîtresse-en-titre. To the embarrassment of all who witnessed the event, she fainted then fled the Court when the king attempted to make the introduction. He is the most genial of monarchs but in no way a milksop. His royal prerogative is paramount. Queen Catherine will remain estranged from Court until she acknowledges Barbara, and in turn, much as Barbara might rail against it, she must smile and bite her tongue if the king makes known his fondness for another."

Despite Franny's reassurance, I trembled from all the attention I was receiving as I sank into my curtsey when King Charles arrived before me. He offered me his hand. I kissed it. He assisted me to rise, kissed the pulse of my wrist, then brushed his lips against mine, an intimate gesture made without passion to signal to those watching that he regarded me as a close friend.

I smiled my gratitude into his eyes. "I find you well this evening, Sire?"

He returned my smile and chuckled. "Od's fish, you do, my naughty lad, even though you appear before me as a lady this evening. Your son, George, and Lady Bonnitta? They are in good spirits?"

King or no, I could have hugged him for remembering their names. "I wrote to them today my excitement of our household being increased by the addition of two puppies."

He nodded. "They will be ready to leave their mama on Friday if you would care to join me at the kennels?"

Joy that gossip of his attention to me would now be the talk of the town, without Franny having to exert the slightest effort on my behalf, bubbled in my belly. "I would be delighted…"

Barbara interjected. "I believe I have no engagements that would prevent me from accompanying you."

The king acquiesced with a small smile in her direction, and I added my part.

"Please, do. They are dear little scamps. Mayhap you would do me the honour of naming them?"

She looked pleased at my offer. The king nodded his satisfaction at the outcome and led her away. I cast a quick glance around the room. Hugo looked in my direction, his gaze steady and a slight smile on his lips. My heart soared, but I didn't meet his eyes, knowing mine would surely give notice of my feelings for him. The Master of Ceremonies further spared my blushes when he invited us to take our seats.

"Your Majesty, my lords, ladies and gentlemen…we are to hear an arrangement played on lute, harpsichord, and madrigals accompanied by a fine castrato newly arrived from the Italian court."

Franny winced. I squeezed his hand then linked my arm through Lady Helen's, and the gentlemen followed on behind us. I settled into my chair, glad of the respite to rein in my feelings for Hugo back into a semblance of composure while I listened.

The male soprano's voice was true and pure, filling the room with awe, though like Franny, much as I enjoyed the performance, I could not help but wonder whether the mutilation needed to produce the sound was not a sacrifice too far. After the last of the applause faded, guests rose from their chairs, and it occurred to me who I had not seen in the ballroom or during the day.

"What has become of Edgeware?"

Franny shrugged. "I did not hear it directly from him, but I believe business has called him away."

I smiled my relief at the news I would not have to keep a wary eye over my shoulder when using the ladies' withdrawing room, then went and did so while keeping an equally nervous eye out for Hugo who I was not at all sure I was ready to come face to face with in a public place.

Mistress Palmer sat before a mirror inspecting her appearance when I exited the private closet.

She turned to face me and spoke using the familiar form of two ladies bearing equal status. "Lady Emma, I believe you must congratulate me, for this morning the king conferred on my husband the honour of Baron Limerick, Earl of Castlemaine, so you now behold Lady Barbara Castlemaine."

An Irish title that, given the poverty of a country ravaged first by the Civil War, then by Cromwell's retribution, I doubted would provide her with any income and as such was not much cause for celebration. What I did not doubt as I looked at the perfection of her face was that it would be the first title of many, and with the aim of my visit to capital accomplished, I saw no point in antagonising a lady who could surely turn the king's opinion against me now she knew what I was about, so I congratulated her anyway.

"I am happy for you, Lady Barbara. May good fortune follow your endeavours and further honours come your way."

Her eyes widened. "I think you mean that."

I reassured her further. "I do, as I did the words I said the other evening. I am honoured to have shared a little private time with His Majesty, and now I have my letter, for my part, therein it ends, though he will always find in me a loyal and loving subject."

She signalled her acceptance of my stance with a gracious smile and rose from her seat. "Then we find ourselves in harmony. Shall we return to the ballroom together?"

I nodded, and she walked alongside me. Faces turned towards us as we entered the room side by side, and the noise increased when the king smiled at the sight of us. We gave each other a brief curtsey then went our separate ways. I reached Franny, and he handed me my wine glass.

"The truce between you and Mistress Palmer is confirmed, my angel?"

I swallowed the last of my wine. "I believe so."

"Then with the king's personal attention to you displayed for all to see, shall we depart and leave the gossipmongers to spread word of it far and wide as they assuredly will once you are absent? Rochester House may prove a pleasant diversion if you would care to dance?"

Seeing several interested persons including Lady Berry and Mistress Blake bearing down on me with questions on their lips, I was nothing loathe. "Yes, but with a quietness? King Charles has not yet taken his leave, and I would not like to give rise to any ill-natured tittle-tattle for my departure taking place before his own and Lady Castlemaine's."

Franny quirked an eyebrow at me. "Lady Castlemaine?"

"As of this morning."

He smirked then offered me his arm. I accepted, and we left our group of friends with their assurances they would follow us shortly, but as we reached the doors to the ballroom, Hugo materialised to one side of me and bowed.

"My lady…?"

My knees trembled. Heat rose to my cheeks, and I found there was nothing I could do about either. I clutched Franny's arm tighter, took a deep breath, and looked at Hugo's forehead rather than his eyes. "It is my happiness to see you here, Mr Fitzwilliam. Are you acquainted with Lord Francombe, my godmother's son?"

They made their bows to each other, and I added to the air over Hugo's head, "My apology I was not at home when you called this morning."

I could not risk exposing myself by looking directly at him, and his next words sounded a little bewildered to my ears.

"May I call on you in the morning? The negotiations for the prospect we have been discussing take place at midday."

I smiled in his general direction and held out my hand. "Would ten of the clock suit you?"

He kissed the back of it. "As ever, I am yours to command, my lady."

I dug the fingernails of my other deeper into Franny's forearm, and a teasing smile lit his face.

"Let us away, my sweet angel. The need to taste wine from the vessel in which your foot currently resides overtakes me. If Mr Fitzwilliam will excuse us?"

He nodded.

Franny led me from the room and said with a soft chuckle, "So that's the way of things between you and your Mr Fitz, is it?"

I stuck my nose in the air. "I have no notion as to what you might be implying, my lord."

Franny laughed louder but refrained from further comment until we were settled side by side in the barge. He flicked my chin with his thumb and forefinger. "So?"

I leaned my head against his shoulder and admitted, "Mr Fitzwilliam has been nothing but concerned for mine and George's welfare. I love him, Franny, but I have no suspicion my feelings are returned. For George's sake, I cannot risk losing him by alerting him that I have a passion for him than exceeds his for me."

Franny squeezed my hand. "From such a brief meeting, I can offer no advice, my sweet. Other than his eyes did not stray from you even though Lady Berry's niece was stood to the side of you simpering as if hoping to attract his notice."

My cheeks heated. "Hugo is a gentleman. He would not slight the lady engaging his attention by gazing past her at another. Miss Berry is attractive and well-connected. I'm sure he was being polite to me, as he always is, while being aware of her charms."

He smiled. "I'm not so sure that is the case, my sweet. He seemed more smitten by you than Miss Berry."

"She is of marriageable age and will have a dowry to match her status. Why would any man take a widow with a young child in preference to that?"

He kissed my shoulder. "Because he loves her."

I thought of the probability, then shook my head. "I've seen no sign of it being so. He is just being kind."

"Time will tell. In the meantime, let us go dance and be as frivolous as we like?"

I smiled up at him. "Yes, my Adonis. Let us set the Town alight with news of our antics."

We disembarked at the Melville residence, and Franny called for a carriage to drive us to Rochester House, and I pushed all thought of Hugo from my head then enjoyed myself enormously until Franny handed me back into the carriage several hours later.

Hannah removed my gown and shooed me into bed when I arrived home. I slept soundly but woke to a ticklish sensation in my midriff at the prospect of Hugo calling on me at ten. I sat up, drank my cocoa, and considered how I could meet him without blushing or acting like a tongue-tied ninny. I brought George to mind, thought of how well Hugo managed the estate on his behalf, and felt sure if I pictured George, I would not give myself away and Hugo would remain at Summerly.

Another of my new gowns had arrived—white taffeta, overlaid with gold lace. It was rather too grand for a day dress, but I donned it anyway, and Franny practically bounced into my sitting room as the hands on the clock neared ten.

"I bear news, my angel. There has been such excitement at the Castlemaine's toilette this morning. It was called early so she may ride out with the royal hunt, and her husband dared to attend, full of pride in his new title. Barbara boxed his ears and sent him from the room with a pithy reminder it was due to her exertions that the honour had been obtained, not his."

I could scarce believe it and giggled. "She didn't? Not in public?"

Franny laughed. "She did, and the king was in attendance."

I narrowed my eyes at him. "Are you jesting me?"

He chuckled. "I am not. I wish you had been with me, for you would have laughed as loud as

I when His Majesty's reaction was to comment, 'And very *fine* exertions they are, indeed.'"

I was still laughing when Hugo's name was announced by a servant, and that being so, found I was relaxed enough to meet his eyes with a smile.

Franny pinched my cheek. "I will leave you to discuss your business, my love. Mama has invited Saltash, Lady Helen, and Exeter to eat their dinner with us tonight. Shall we say the Tapestry room at seven?"

I blew him a kiss. "I will be nothing but delighted, my Adonis."

He turned to Hugo. "And you, sir? The Duchess of Melville would be delighted to receive you, as I would be honoured to further our acquaintance?"

Hugo bowed. "The honour would be mine, my lord."

Franny left. I offered Hugo the back of my hand, and though my heart thumped at the touch of his lips, I was relieved to see it did not tremble. I gestured towards the consul table once he released it.

"Would you care to pour us a glass of sherry-wine?"

He handed me the small casket he carried and did as I'd suggested. I sat and looked at the box. Highly lacquered and decorated with painted pink roses, it was of a size to contain gloves or maybe feathers to adorn a hat. He set my wine down on the side table within reach of my hand, then sat on the sofa opposite me.

"It contains what I hope you'll agree is a good investment opportunity."

Intrigued, I lifted the lid and saw squares of a pink-and-white something, dusted with fine white powder.

"It is a confection. Would you care to taste it?"

I picked up a pink square, bit down, and a sweetness more intense than any I had experienced before filled my mouth. It was wonderful. Almond marchpane and dried fruits coated with sticky honey paled into insignificance as I swallowed. "Oh my!"

Hugo smiled. "Presented in such a pretty manner it could be the latest sensation, don't you think? I can see boxes of it sitting on the occasional tables of every lady in the land."

My mouth still watering, I gasped. "What is it?"

Hugo's smile widened. "A new concoction from France. The recipe is spelt n-o-u-g-a-t, but the French pronounce it nou-gaar. The method to create it is not complicated but requires a great deal of sugar, and a large quantity of that particular commodity is being auctioned at midday."

I thought back to the conversation I had had with Franny. "From Queen Catherine's dowry?"

He looked pleased at my guessing. "Yes. There is such a glut the price is as low as I can scarce believe it. Stored correctly, sugar does not deteriorate or spoil. I am hoping to purchase enough to ensure us a substantial profit for several years to come."

I noted the gleam in his eyes. "How much of the shipment will we be purchasing?"

He smiled. "All of it, I hope. I have men stationed on the dockside to place bids on the individual lots to ensure the price is not driven upwards by some enterprising person who suspects my plan. The purchases will appear laconic and random as they should be when such a surplus of a commodity is for sale."

I clapped my hands together, excited at the prospect of his plans coming to fruition. "Oh, I would like to view that event. May I accompany you?"

The smile left his face, and his cheeks tinged pink. "Ah... Docks are dirty places, my lady. I fear your gown would never recover its elegance. Females, excepting fishwives, are never seen there."

Much as I appreciated his concern, his challenge stirred me, so I picked up my glass and swallowed its contents down in one large chug. His eyes widened, and a small bubble of glee fizzled in my belly.

"If you will give me ten minutes, sir. We shall see what may be done about that."

I didn't wait for his answer but stood and hastened to my dressing room. Hannah was inside it, mending a chemise.

I pulled the ribbons from my hair. "My male attire in double-quick time, if you please. And tie my hair at the nape of my neck in the same manner as Mr Fitzwilliam does when he rides out at Summerly."

I looked at the time when I reentered the sitting room. In eight minutes, Hannah had worked wonders. I smiled brightly at Hugo.

"So, how long will it take us to reach the docks? I imagine we should leave immediately?"

I was delighted at the expression of surprise on his face, although he quickly recovered and stood.

"We should."

I tucked my arm through his, and he glanced sideways at me as we walked through the garden towards the wherry pier.

"Where did you obtain the male clothing?"

I laughed. "Franny took me to his tailor."

"Franny…? That would be Viscount Francombe, I presume?"

I noted his hesitation so answered his underlying question. "It is, and I love Franny dearly. He has been wonderful to me since I arrived at my godmother's, though his affections are engaged elsewhere."

Hugo's shoulders relaxed. "It is sometimes difficult to tell given the easy manners in the capital these days."

Arms linked, we sauntered on.

"It is, but I prefer it to when I accompanied Earl Summerly here during the time of the Commonwealth."

He smiled. "When you halted at the coaching inn at Bedford in bad weather, then the downpour eased, and the sun came out?"

I smiled at the memory of George's wonder when a magnificent rainbow had appeared on the horizon. "Yes. How did you know?"

He stepped aboard the barge. "You were preoccupied in soothing your husband when

177

George became animated at the sight of so many colours in the sky, so did not look out of the carriage, but awaiting a change of horse myself, I was there."

Memories of the early years of my marriage flooded into my mind. George hungry. George crying. The rest of the household regarding me with sorrowful eyes as they surveyed their rations of bread and water because I had been caught smiling, or worse, found laughing with my white linen cap askew. Contradiction of my husband's edicts, he considered an indecent breach of my feminine virtue, and to ensure the depth of his revulsion was understood, retribution was meted out to all. Still, that particular day, I'd come within a hair's breadth of expressing my displeasure at his unreasonable expectation that a three-year-old child should be quiet at all times.

"I so nearly took him to task for his impatience but managed to hold my tongue."

"I always wondered at your ability to do so."

A shiver ran down my spine. "If it had been only myself to face the consequences of displeasing him, I would not have been so compliant, but I could not see the household put on short rations because of my misdemeanour—

especially when the punishment included my son."

Hugo's voice sounded revolted. "He refused food to a young child?"

I stepped aboard the wherry and perched on the bench seat. "You knew him, Hugo. He was an irritable curmudgeon. Once George was weaned from his wet nurse, he was deemed as answerable as the rest of us."

If I didn't agree with Hugo, my cheeks would have turned pink at the fierceness of his response.

"Od's blood! Some men are unfit to be named Father!"

"I try not to dwell on it. He has no power over me now, no more does the Duke of Portchester. King Charles is the kindest of men. I have his written assurance any concern I hold for George's and Bonnie's well-being he will make his also."

He sat beside me. "I noticed His Majesty seemed rather attentive to you last evening. I hope his favour hasn't placed you in an uncomfortable position?"

I took a deep breath and admitted what I refused to hide even though he might think less of me for doing so. "I am in no position I didn't actively seek."

His shoulders stiffened. "You sought?"

I huffed my exasperation. "What lengths you would go to, Hugo? To protect your family when those seeking to take advantage of them are the very people in whom you should be able to place your trust? Widowed and alone, the only way for me to trounce a duke is to trump him with a king."

The barge halted at the jetty, and I leapt onto it. He joined me after paying the wherryman and disembarking from the craft with rather more dignity than I had displayed.

"My apologies. It is not my business to enquire, other than does this mean you will be prolonging your sojourn in the capital to stay at Court, my lady?"

I ignored his return to formal manners and tucked my arm through his. "Absolutely not. I have no intention of becoming any further embroiled in the mad dance that surrounds the king. Myself, my letter, George, and Bonnie will be returning home to Summerly just as soon as I receive the puppies he gifted me from the royal litter."

His expression lightened. "Puppies, my lady? George and Bonnie will like that, I should think. They have never been permitted a house pet to date, have they?"

Happy not to be at odds with him, I smiled. "Call me by my name, Hugo. You can't be *my ladying* me all over the docks when I'm dressed as a boy."

"Then I can't call you Emma, either. You'll have to be Emry or something."

"Emry it is then."

We walked towards a warehouse in front of which a wooden dais had been constructed. A crowd of men were gathered looking expectedly at it, and Hugo's impressive size made short work of parting a path for us to make our way through it.

He bent his head close to my ear. "If you glance around you will recognise the Summerly men."

I did so, not resting my gaze for too long in any one place as if I were merely interested in observing the spectacle. I saw four of my tenant farmers, along with Egbert, the miller, and Cuthbert, Hugo's body servant—all men educated enough to be able to reckon their numbers and sign their name.

I murmured back, "A good choice."

Two men came out of the warehouse and mounted the dais, one I presumed to be the auctioneer, and William Chiffinch, who sat at a table with a ledger on it.

The auctioneer began by bellowing, "Gentlemen, your attention please."

The crowd quietened.

"The lots will be of equal size, each containing two hundred barrels. Given the debacle of the spice auction afore this, heed my words. I will not be standing here all day whilst you bicker, so not waste my time by trying to split the lots between yourselves piecemeal. If you cannot meet the price for the quantity, do not bid. There will be no sub-dividing."

Hugo expressed his satisfaction at the ripple of restless muttering around us. "Good. That should put paid to the ambitions of more than half this crowd."

The first lot was called, and the winning bid was placed by Cuthbert who made his way to the dais to sign his name and promise of payment in Chiffinch's ledger. By the time Hugo raised his hand to bid on the last lot of the day, Chiffinch was doing a reckoning on his abacas and smiling broadly.

The crowd dispersed until only myself, Hugo, the Summerly men, and Chiffinch remained.

Chiffinch raised his eyes from his ledger. "Approach please, gentlemen, and tell me how and when your payment will be made."

Hugo pulled a pouch of coins from his pocket and handed it to Cuthbert. "With my thanks, refresh yourselves with food and ale at old Mother Shipton's tavern, and I will join you when our business is complete."

I walked with Hugo to the dais where Chiffinch looked most perturbed to see his buyers disappearing. "Do they not realise their bids are binding?"

"They do, sir," Hugo said. "But they were bidding on behalf of the Summerly Estate, and the seventy thousand crowns owed by them and myself will be delivered to the Treasury in the morning."

He signed to that effect in the ledger, and Chiffinch's smile returned.

"Lady Emma, you are not here merely for your entertainment? You have purchased the entire cargo?"

I glanced up at Hugo's satisfied expression. "I rather think we have."

Chiffinch closed his ledger and jumped to his feet. "I must away and tell the king. He'll be delighted. I'll admit he didn't expect more than half to be sold for there was so much of the wretched stuff, and as ever, the Exchequer is in need of funds."

He walked away, then turned back around with a slight frown. "What will you do with it all?"

I smiled. "Mr Fitzwilliam has an excellent scheme in mind."

His brow cleared. "Fitzwilliam? Of course. Forgive me, sir, for being a little tense and therefore not acknowledging your name when you signed. Your family has ever been generous in the support of King Charles and his late father. I should have known this happy circumstance would have been bought about by a true supporter."

Hugo bowed. "Hugo, the younger FitzWilliam, at your service, sir, and the deal is not altogether altruistic but beneficial to both parties, I believe. For we do indeed have a plan in mind for the commodity purchased."

Chaffinch rubbed his hands together. "Good, good. A profitable day all round then."

I tucked my arm through Hugo's. "So, Mother Shipton's tavern? Does it serve tankards of dark brew? If so, I think I had best eat a slice of pie or something before I drink it. I felt quite woozy for not having eaten when Fanny took me on a tour of the ale houses."

Hugo grinned, something he did not do often, and it lit his face. "Boys clothes and ale houses? Is there anything further you wish to shock me with today?"

I laughed. "Yes. I attended Lady Castlemaine's Grand Toilette while pretending to be male and also visited the theatre in a gold ballgown then sat in the Pit."

"Emry! What has become of you since you arrived in London?"

"Do you not like it?"

He looked into my eyes, his own as warm and green as set my heart racing. "I like it very much."

I smiled, and we walked on. Fish scales and rotting guts underfoot made our path precarious, but despite the stench, I enjoyed clutching Hugo's arm when I skidded on the slime. He grinned every time I near lost my balance, and I thought our contact delighted him as much as it did me.

Chapter Nine

W e left the docks, and the cobbles became firmer, though the odour did not become any pleasanter when the stink of the midden joined it. He pushed open the door of the second building we came to, and I inhaled smoking tallow and the smell of ale with some relief.

The Summerly men were gathered around a table at the back of the room. A serving girl set a plate of victuals down in front of Cuthbert and pressed her breasts against his back. He saw me watching, blushed, and waved her away.

I pulled a chair forward as I reached them and sat. "She is a working girl. You are a working man. If you find each other's company agreeable, do not shun her on my behalf, if you please."

Hugo stood behind me and placed his hands on my shoulders. I found I couldn't help it and tilted my head backwards to rest on his muscled midriff while wondering what he looked like naked.

His hands squeezed a little. "I second the countess. Well done, men. None of you are committed elsewhere. Enjoy all the tavern has to offer."

He assisted me to rise and tucked my arm through his. "I think we should leave them to it and seek our refreshment elsewhere."

I nodded my agreement, and we walked to the next ale house. Hugo ordered us a pie apiece and two tankards. I chugged my ale once it arrived, swiped the foam from my upper lip, and asked the question that had been loitering in my mind since Chiffinch had mentioned the matter on the dais. "So, you are aware of my circumstances during the Interregnum. How did your family fare?"

He lifted his tankard. "King Henry was my great-great-grandfather. My lineage descends from his mistress, Bessie Blount, and the son she bore him, Henry Fitzroy, Duke of Grafton. Illegitimate and three times removed, my family's claim to royalty is tenuous at best, but Cromwell considered us a possible rallying point for the Royalist cause. We were placed under house arrest in the household of General Fairfax, although my father managed to escape and fled to the Continent to join the king in exile. M'mother, brother, and I were released on Cromwell's death, and m'father returned to us at the time of the king's coronation."

"How were you treated by the general? I've heard he is an honourable man."

Hugo nodded. "Apart from the loss of liberty, we were treated fairly. Lord Fairfax might have been a fervent believer that Parliament should be more than a mere cipher of the king, but he was also opposed to the country being governed by military rule. He refused to attend the trial of the king's father and did his best to avert his eventual execution."

"And that's why he's been pardoned and allowed to retire on a pension?"

"That and also for his part in negotiating our king's restoration to the throne."

I swallowed the last of my ale and Hugo the last of his pie.

"We'd best be off, Emry. You need to change into Emma, and I need to ensure your strongbox contains the correct quantity of crowns."

I followed him from the tavern. We stepped aboard a wherry and disembarked at the Melville residence. He continued his journey by foot, onwards to his father's London house with his assurance he would return promptly at seven.

Hannah bustled out of the dressing room and bobbed her curtsey as I let myself into my rooms.

"My lady, another of your new gowns arrived this afternoon if you would care to view it?"

I poured myself a small glass of sherry-wine. "I would, if you please."

She bought me a gown that near took my breath away. Gold lace spotted all over with tiny beads of amber which glistened as they caught the light.

I smiled. "'Tis beautiful. If you would fetch my washing water?"

She did so then, ahead of time, I twirled in front of the looking glass and hoped Hugo would *very much* like the sight of me wearing it. I sat on sofa with the remainder of my sherry to await the appointed time to descend downstairs, and a tap sounded on the sitting room door. I nodded to Hannah to open it, wondering who it could be— my friends would be in their own homes dressing in their evening attire, Franny always bounced into my rooms without knocking, and my godmother had never visited past the day she had shown them to me.

My comfort did not increase when she opened it and Uncle John glowered on the threshold. I took a deep breath and stood so he did not have the advantage of looming over me.

"How delightful of you to find the time to visit me here, Your Grace. Such another unexpected surprise."

He banged the door shut in the face of the pageboy who had shown him up and strode farther into the room, his angry gaze raking me from top to bottom. "'Tis true, then? Everything Edgeware said? I would scarce believe it if your shame wasn't on display before my eyes. You have deserted your home, hearth, and child to become a strumpeting lollygag."

I gritted my teeth. "Edgeware?"

"Was so concerned as to the depth of moral turpitude to which you have sunk, felt he had no choice but to hasten to my side and beg for my intervention before you become any further embroiled in a life of vice."

"Two-faced shakeragg!"

His eyes bulged. "You dare to utter such foulness for a man who only has your best interests at heart? Well, I will not stand for it, madam. I have taken control of Summerly. My men are in place, and Mr Fitzwilliam can consider himself dismissed. The young earl's affairs will in future be managed by me."

Blood pounded through my veins, and for the first time I did not buckle under his intimidation. I unlocked my jewel box and offered him my letter from King Charles along with my forthright refusal to comply with his instructions. "You will *not* be doing so, Your Grace. I am returning home to Summerly next week and I had best *not* find either you, *nor* any of your retainers, on my son's estate."

He snatched the letter from my hand, and his cheeks reddened as he perused the contents. "You will regret this, you conniving Jezebel!"

I plucked my precious missive from his fingers. "I give you good evening, Your Grace.

You are not welcome here, and do not visit Summerly again without giving due notice and receiving my written permission you may do so."

He turned on his heel, crashed the door into its frame, and I gulped down the rest of my wine.

Hannah smiled. "Your mother would have been proud, my lady. His Grace is a bully, and she stood her ground against him whenever she could, even if your father pleaded with her not to."

The clock chimed seven. I set down my glass then left my rooms and found Franny at the foot of the stairs, staring at his front doors.

"Is that who I suspect it is, my sweet?"

"Yes. The Duke of Portchester, otherwise known as my Uncle John."

His eyes sparkled as comprehension dawned. "And you dispatched him sure in the knowledge your affairs are no longer any of his business?"

I grinned in a most unladylike way. "He was somewhat less than delighted at the change of circumstances."

Franny laughed. "And how did your business progress with Mr FitzWilliam, my love?"

"Very well, I believe. We attended an auction at the docks and purchased a great deal of sugar which we are going to turn into nou-gaar."

"What is nou-gaar?"

I smiled. "An extraordinary confection newly arrived from France. Visit my rooms in the morning and take a taste. Hugo bought some with him."

He grinned and winked. "Hugo, is it now?"

My cheeks heated, which only made him laugh louder.

My godmother sat me beside Franny at dinner with Madam Blake to his other side. Hugo she placed opposite, though much farther along the table with Miss Berry on his left and her mother to his right.

As if noticing where my gaze had rested, Madame Blake leaned closer and confided in a low voice, "If the fluttering eyelashes are anything to go by, I think Miss Julia may be enamoured. The duchess told me Lady Berry called this afternoon and practically begged for them to be invited this evening. I wonder by what means she discovered he was on the guest list?"

I feigned bored disinterest. "I have no idea." Which I didn't, what with Hugo being in my company for most of the day, until I noticed Franny looking a little sheepish.

I waited until Madame Blake turned away then nudged his knee with mine. "Well?"

He murmured, "You must not hold me at fault, my sweet. I was quite artfully pumped for information regarding Mr Fitzwilliam in the Privy Gardens this morning." He glanced at Lady Berry. "Though with the absence of her daughter simpering at her side to give the game away, I did not realise it at the time."

I stroked my fingertips down his cheek and played the game to Madam Blake's round-eyed stare. "As ever, you are forgiven, my beautiful Adonis."

He pulled my hand to his lips and kissed into the center of my palm. "Most gorgeous star in the heavens above, as ever, my heart rejoices at your words."

Lady Helen, sitting opposite us beside her brother, giggled, and he chimed in with his part in the farce.

"Golden Goddess, before whom the midday orb blushes, shine your attention on me, I beg."

I smirked my appreciation of his playful banter. "My lord, you will be demanding the ruination of my footwear next. I know it!"

Those of us privy to the jest, including Exeter and Rochester, laughed and, surrounded by my friends, I felt more comfortable to glance towards the giggled titters emanating from Miss Julia. Hugo met my gaze, and knowing his expressions well, I recognised the sign of boredom in his eyes. My mood lightened, and I was able to eat my dinner in comfort.

Hugo escaped the Berry's after the final course and made his way to my side. "The Summerly strongbox is secured at m'father's London house, but I have to admit I will not rest easy until that quantity of crowns is safely delivered to the Treasury in the morning."

I confided my own fears. "The Duke of Portchester called on me before dinner. When the gold is receipted and acknowledged, send the Summerly men to Hatfield for George's and Bonnie's protection, if you please?"

His irises darkened. "He threatened them?"

"Not as such, but he attempted to take control of the estate which I've forestalled by means of the king's letter. He has no sure knowledge of their whereabouts, but I would feel happier to know our own men are close by."

He bowed. "Be assured of it. I will call on you when all is accomplished."

I offered the back of my hand for his kiss, and he seemed as reluctant to release it as I was to take it away, then, once he departed, I floated through the rest of the evening as if walking on air.

Franny was the first to enter my sitting room the following day. "I give you a good morn, my angel. Rochester's company was so sweet overnight it has left me with a longing to taste your nou-gaar."

I opened the box and offered him a piece.

Hugo was shown in as Franny's eyes widened while he spluttered, "Zounds!"

I exchanged a smile with Hugo. "Another success, I think."

"As it is with our other concerns also. Payment has been made, and the Summerly men ride to Hatfield as we speak."

Franny swallowed his mouthful. "Do you have any more boxes of the confection with you? If so, you should consider presenting them to ladies of influence in the Town. I am sure my mother would appreciate such a delicacy and would recommend it to her friends, which, mayhap, would begin to set a trend?"

Hugo agreed. "An excellent notion. That I do, though only another three samples."

"In the company of King Charles and Lady Castlemaine, I am visiting the royal kennels on the morrow. I could gift her a box when I receive the puppies?"

Franny nodded. "Yes, but you should also offer a box to the king. If his mistress already possesses the treat, who else will he pass it on to but the queen he is trying to get enceinte?"

Hugo agreed. "A queen, the king's premier mistress, a duchess, and a countess. An excellent start to our campaign."

I asked, "My box is incomplete so cannot be gifted to another. I will offer the nou-gaar around the room at the next card evening I attend here, but how complicated is the process to create it? If the confection is liked, how soon can we get more?"

Hugo warmed to his theme. "That is the beauty of it. Though the utmost care is needed when heating the sugar, only water and whisked egg white comprise the rest. The village goodwives can produce it in their cottage kitchens to earn extra coin. Their menfolk can create the caskets in the evening to supplement their income. A well-fed belly works harder, so each cottager will receive a dozen chickens, and the yolks not required to make the confection can be scrambled or coddled to feed the family. With three large villages and a small township within the boundaries of the Summerly estate, I estimate at least a thousand caskets can be made and filled each week."

Franny looked a little stunned. "That is quite some enterprise, sir. Sugar is a valuable commodity. Can you be sure your villagers will not be tempted to retain a portion for themselves and sell it on?"

Hugo nodded. "Overseers will be appointed to ensure the quantity of nou-gaar created matches the amount of sugar given and weigh the output lest any enterprising person thinks to alter the ratio of sugar to egg white, but now, before I turn into a complete bore, I will desist speaking of it."

"No, sir. Do not think it," Franny answered. "I will admit I have no head for business, but the principle of mutual cooperation to create additional wealth for all will be of interest to m'father, I'm sure. If you would permit me to outline the principle to him?"

Hugo bowed. "Of course, and should he require any further detail, I will supply it."

Franny thanked him, and with an appointment to see his tailor at noon, wished us farewell and left the room.

I looked at Hugo. "I thank you for setting my mind at ease. Do not let me detain you if you have other matters that should be occupying your time?"

He smiled. "I don't as it happens. It is a beautiful day. Would you care to take an outing to the park?"

I threaded my arm through his with eager alacrity. "That I would."

The sun was still as warm as it had been all month, and there was little sign that given the time of the year, the weather should be autumnal. We walked away from the river, and two heavily laden wagons containing hewn blocks of Portland stone rumbled past us.

Hugo watched them move into the distance. "'Tis destined for the new terrace of townhouses being built at Westminster. The water contains more effluent with each passing year, so m'father commissioned one of them. He believes, in a few years, the most desirable properties will stand back from the river."

I thought back to my conversation with Franny. "That being the case, the waterfront property that is so damp as to be uninhabitable, should we sell it and invest elsewhere for George? Rochester is interested in purchasing the land."

Hugo considered the matter then nodded. "If the price offered is sufficient, yes. Perhaps you would like to view the terrace? M'father's property was the first constructed."

His invitation thrilled me. Hugo was at Summerly most days, but he had turned down my late husband's offer to accommodate him in the house, understandably, given the miserable atmosphere that permeated the place during my spouse's lifetime. Instead, he had purchased a hunting lodge some three miles distant and, never having had a reasonable excuse to call by, I had never been inside it. The prospect of glimpsing any place Hugo called home was irresistible, though I didn't let my excitement show.

"On George's behalf, yes, perhaps I should. When would you suggest?"

He smiled. "If we take the path south around the edge of the park, we will come across them in not so many minutes."

The park was crowded with sightseers, as it always was if the royal hunting party was known to be within it. Hugo greeted as many acquaintances as I, although they belonged to a different set to Franny's friends, so I did not know them. Hugo paused here and there to introduce me and, having not had the opportunity to do so the previous evening, I did the same when we came across Lady Helen and Exeter strolling arm in arm.

She glanced at Exeter and blushed a little. "We are having a reception at Saltash House tonight at nine. Will you attend?"

I guessed the reason. "To celebrate your betrothal?"

Her colour deepened. "Yes. It will not be a large gathering, given Mama's health is not of the best, but do come if you are not promised elsewhere."

I assured them nothing could keep me away, and Exeter smiled broadly.

"And you, sir? We'd be delighted to welcome any friend of Lady Emma's if you have no prior engagement?"

Hugo bowed his thanks for the invitation. "I promised to join m'father for dinner at six, but as he does not linger overlong at the table, I would be confident of being able to attend your party by nine."

Exeter bowed his respects in return. "Excellent! Join us when you will, sir. No rush, no rush."

We left them, walked on, and Hugo tucked my arm tighter through his at the sight of Lady Berry and her daughter up ahead.

Her face wreathed in smiles, she hurried towards us and cooed, "Mr FitzWilliam. What a happiness to see you here. You must come and eat your supper with us tonight. We will have games afterwards and play hide and seek and blind man's bluff if all promise not to be too saucy about it."

He did not let go of my arm to make his bow but merely tipped his head. "Impossible, I'm afraid. I am otherwise engaged."

Lady Julia fluttered her eyelashes and peeked coyly upwards at Hugo. "Oh, *do* come. It will be *such* fun."

He glanced at me, and I nearly laughed out loud at the gleam of horrified disbelief in his eyes until Lady Julia added, "I'm sure Lady Emma will excuse you."

Having given her no leave to use my Christian name, I stared her down until she blushed for her ill manners, then rescued Hugo. "Mr FitzWilliam and I are promised to attend a gathering at

Saltash House this evening. It is not an invitation to be reneged on in favour of attending an impromptu romp. I give a good day to you both."

We walked on past them, and Hugo shuddered.

"Do I look like the type of man who would indulge in a game of hide and seek?"

I tried to picture him concealed behind a half-open door then running pell-mell back to base while being pursued by a giggling Miss Berry and laughed. "No, you do not, though I can see Miss Julia would be enchanted to come across you in a secluded corner."

"As I have never been known to skulk in nooks and crannies, she will not do so, and I will admit, this growing fashion for adults to play childhood games after dinner embarrasses me."

"I can't say I've attended any dinner where such games were played, only cards, but I've enjoyed my stay with my godmother, though I would leif not live here permanently like she and Franny do. The pleasure of company and entertainment would pall for me if I stayed overlong, I believe. Better to come and go at will."

He nodded his agreement, and a row of houses came into view. Each was not of a dissimilar size to my godmother's, but they stood side by side with no land in between them. Four buildings looked to be complete with another five rising from behind wooden scaffolding interspersed with block and tackle to hoist the squares of Portland stone upwards to be cemented into place.

Hugo paused before the first of them. Several steps ascended to the front entrance situated under a canopy, and I followed him up them. He opened the door and took a step backwards so I could precede him.

The pageboy sitting just inside it jumped to his feet when he saw us and bowed. "Mr Hugo, sir."

Hugo waved him down. "As you were, Tom."

I looked around and was impressed. A marble staircase rose in front of me, and the hall I was standing in was light, airy, and contained several highly polished wooden doors. Hugo as a younger son might have to make his own way in the world, but this was obviously the residence of a wealthy man.

Hugo took my hand. "The public rooms are on this floor, those necessary for the house to function in the basement beneath us, our private apartments are above, and sleeping quarters for the staff in the attic space." He opened the first door.

I peeked in at a library. The next he opened showed a dining room, and two more revealed less formal rooms for the use of the ladies. Each was of more than generous proportions, and that included a magnificent ballroom that ran full-length across the back of the house.

I gazed out of one of its floor-to-ceiling windows at the gardens. The house faced directly onto the street, but to the back was a large, green cultivated space laid to lawn with lavender and rose bushes intersecting its length.

"'Tis lovely. Perfect for entertaining when visiting the capital."

Hugo smiled. "M'mother is not fond of visiting London, so many of the rooms are never used. It's more of a bachelor arrangement at present. Minimal servants…that type of thing."

The door opened. Cuthbert walked in and seemed more taken aback to find me standing in the FitzWilliam family home than he had seeing me dressed as a boy on the dockside the previous day.

"Ah…beggin' your pardon, sir, but Tom said as you were home. Dinner with the Baron is in less than an hour."

Hugo took out his pocket watch. "So it is. Dispatch Tom to flag down a Hackney so I may escort the countess to the Melville residence, if you would."

I smiled then offered him a release from his obligation if the time until his next engagement was short. "Tom could accompany me in your place?"

Hugo waited for Cuthbert to leave the room. "Golden goddess, how likely do you think it is I would trust a ten-year-old boy to fend off your admirers if you are out in public with only him at your side?"

My heart raced at the warmth in his eyes. "Flowery phrases, Hugo? A new addition to your repertoire?"

Straight-faced, but with a teasing glint in his eye, he answered, "When stolen from those more eloquent, I am shameless in my thievery, oh star of the heavens above."

I sighed loudly and japed him back. "Oh my! Such phraseology. Dear sir, you overwhelm me!"

He laughed and offered me his arm. We walked to the front doors, but before we reached them, they opened to admit another gentleman. Apart from the greying hair, the resemblance was so obvious as to leave me in no doubt I beheld Hugo's sire. I withdrew my arm for Hugo to make the introduction, which he did.

"Father, may I present the Countess of Summerly."

I dipped a polite courtesy, and he hurried forward as I straightened while giving Hugo a pointed stare over my shoulder that promised an explanation would be demanded later.

"My lady, I am honoured…"

I did what I could to soothe him. "As am I. Your son has been so kind as to show me the superior quality of the houses currently under construction away from the waterfront. Our own property is damp, inhospitable, and boasts no such facilities as are on offer here."

Baron FitzWilliam bowed. "Then I will add my assurance to that of my son. These properties are a sound investment…more solid than anything built of wattle and daub."

I smiled and laid my hand back on Hugo's forearm. He escorted me out and handed me into the carriage of a two-horse Hackney. I thought of my late husband's first wife and the age of Hugo's father, which although not contemporary, was close enough. I settled against the squabs and asked as Hugo joined me, "He doesn't know I'm Caroline's replacement?"

Hugo frowned. "I never gave it a thought before today, but m'father was in exile for so

208

long, he might not know she died and Earl Summerly remarried."

I smiled. "Understandable then, especially given neither I nor my late husband ever left the Summerly Estate since your father's return to England."

The Hackney pulled up under the portico of the Melville residence, and Hugo handed me out with his hope to meet me at Saltash House later.

Franny walked into my rooms as I was standing in front of my clothes press choosing a gown. "Such wonderful news of the betrothal, my angel. You are privy to it, I presume?"

I kissed his cheek. "Indeed, I am. What should I wear? Lady Helen's wardrobe is not extensive, and she should be the belle of her own betrothal party."

He pointed towards a cream silk day dress, plain but elegant. "If accompanied by jewels and a gold net petticoat, mayhap this one would meet your colour scheme?"

I suspected Lady Helen would select a dress I had gifted to her, which, pretty as they were, did not have the luxurious touch of a true evening gown, so smiled my agreement. Hannah plucked my choice from between those vying for its attention, laid it over the back of a chair, and trotted off to fetch hot water.

Franny kissed the back of my hand. "With apologies, my sweet. Mine own attendance is required at Whitehall by the king this evening, so I cannot escort you. I suspect having received his due reward from Lady Castlemaine in appreciation of her new title, he is in the mood to enjoy a little high jinks away from the palace."

In the expectation of seeing only friends at Saltash House, I felt quite comfortable to arrive there unescorted. "I will be acquainted with many of the guests this evening, thanks to you. I shall travel in a closed carriage driven by mine own Silas Coachman, sure of finding agreeable company when I arrive."

He smiled. "I still intend to offer my congratulations in person. There will be ample opportunity to excuse myself for a time in between ale houses, I'm sure."

I called for my coach when dinner was complete, and several friends were in the Long

Gallery when I arrived, although to my disappointment, not Hugo. King Charles appeared with several of his courtiers, including Franny, around ten, and a surprised hum ran round the room. The company bowed or curtsied, and he invited us to rise with any airy flick of his hand.

"No formality, if you please. Given the occasion, I could not resist stopping by for a few minutes."

They looked delighted at the honour being paid by his personal visit, and as he gave them his blessing to their union, Franny appeared at my side.

I knocked his elbow with mine. "How did you manage it?"

He smirked. "'Twas not difficult once he knew of it, my angel. Both families always supported the Royalist cause. Our Sovereign is not so high above himself that he will not give credit where it's due."

I had no reason to doubt Franny's words after the king left them, paused in front of me, and kissed the pulse of my wrist.

"Lady Emma, I hear you have been refilling my Treasury."

I curtsied my respects. "I cannot take the credit for it, Your Highness. 'Tis Summerly coinage, but the scheme was devised by Mr Hugo FitzWilliam."

"The younger of the baron's sons?"

I nodded, and he brushed his lips along mine. "I do not see him at Court so very often, but I will thank him when I do. In the meantime, I shall meet you at the royal kennels on the morrow?"

The thought of receiving the two dear little pups I'd selected delighted me. "That you will, Sire, if they are ready to leave their mama?"

He smiled. "That they are."

It occurred to me that the king had spent more minutes with me than any other, so I took a step backwards to release him from the obligation of conversing with me for any longer.

He lifted my hand to his lips. "I shall arrange the timing."

I watched him depart and was not totally surprised when a pageboy approached me a few minutes later. "His Majesty requests a minute or two your time before his coach departs, my lady."

I gave my glass to Lord Saltash. "In regard to the hour of my visit to the royal kennels, I should think."

Chapter Ten

I made my way to the vestibule and nodded to the footmen standing to each side of the double front doors. They opened one a piece and bowed me out. I stepped over the threshold. The back of a coach halted a few paces past the flaming flambeaux illuminating the frontage of Saltash House. I walked closer but hesitated when I realised what I wasn't seeing was the Royal Coat of Arms painted on its door. The coach appeared to be a little 'too quiet' to my eyes, but as it was not unknown for King Charles to travel incognito if engaged on his own private entertainment in Town, I peered through the gloom, not wishing to offend if it was him.

No sign of a boisterous bachelor party inside the vehicle greeted my closer inspection, so I half turned, poised for flight, then cursed delaying my departure as a figure clad in dark clothing detached from the shadows and grabbed my upper arms in a vice-like grip.

I tried to pull away to an amused sneer. "Did I not warn you I would get my way, madam?"

I kicked out at the detested voice. "You…"

Edgeware did not so much as flinch, and I realised he was wearing leather riding boots rather than silk stockings and shoes.

He tugged me closer. "You can thank Lady Berry for the gossip you would be here this evening as I thank His Majesty for attending and giving me plausible excuse to call you from the room. Not that you wouldn't have been intercepted on your way home had this opportune moment not arrived."

I tried to twist away. "Desist, my lord. Whatever funds my uncle promised were destined to come under your control should you marry me are no more. I have the king's written assurance in the matter."

His fingers dug in harder. "So your uncle informed me yesterday. Irritating...but still you have value to me in that you have spawned a healthy male child. If you can do so for an elderly man, you will surely do so for a one more vigorous."

I turned my shoulders this way and that, straining to free myself from his grasp. "I will never willingly submit to you."

"Which will only make the fruit of your eventual surrender sweeter to my taste."

I raised my knee towards his groin. "You will beget a bastard, then. For I assure you, the required responses of the marriage service shall not pass from my lips."

He swerved my attack as if expecting it. "Do you suppose your uncle and I did not consider the matter when he arrived at my door frothing with anger last evening? He agrees with my opinion. You are treading a ruinous path and must be saved from the consequences of your own actions, by force if necessary."

"You hypocritical whoreson!"

He laughed, and it was not a pleasant sound. "According to the Duke of Portchester, I am your saviour, and you are to be confined to the rotunda at my hunting lodge until you come to your senses and marry me. There will be no paper, no ink, nor any other avenue for you to appeal to the king, as not another soul bar us will know you are there. Now, get into the coach."

He clasped me in a bear hug so tight I could barely breathe and hustled me towards the vehicle, and panic set in when awareness of the true danger of my situation dawned. In desperation, I gathered all the breath I had left and let out a screech in the hope that someone, anyone would hear me.

"Help! Kidnap! Help me!"

My eyes filled with tears of relief at the sound fast-moving footsteps and Hugo's voice.

"I believe the lady has more than adequately expressed her reluctance to depart in your company, sir. Unhand her at once, or I will take her from you, and you will answer to me the justification of your actions at dawn-break on the morrow."

I blinked tears away as Hugo strode closer, his face rigid with anger, taller and broader in every way than the man threatening me. His thunderous expression left no room for doubt my assailant would be pummelled into mincemeat if he did not comply. Edgeware loosened his grip, then shoved me forcefully towards Hugo with a suddenness I was not expecting.

"Take the bitch then! For without the annual income I was expecting, her womb is not worth the price of risking my life."

I stumbled. Hugo hissed and stepped forward to stop my fall, so I did what any self-respecting heroine worth her salt would do and swooned gracefully into his arms. He caught me as I had hoped and shot a look of pure venom towards Edgeware.

"You, sir, are a disgrace and a coward to boot. Get you gone from here."

Edgeware moved towards his coach. "My father has influence at Court. Should I discover you have been blackening my reputation…"

Hugo cut him off, his voice low and furious. "I would not soil my lady's name by mentioning your abominable behaviour in the same breath. Slink away, Sirrah, for you are no Gentleman of Honour but a whey-faced poltroon!"

The full consequences of my sudden vanishing worked their way into my mind, and shivers ran through my body. My personal revulsion at the thought of enforced intimacy with Edgeware aside, George and Bonnie would have been left bewildered and helpless at my disappearance. They would have been forced to return to Summerly. I was sure Hugo would have sent out urgent enquiries, but had I been imprisoned securely with no method of contacting the king, no word would have returned. In the face of that, my warrant to him could not have held.

He held me tighter while I shook. "There, there, my love. You are safe now."

I rested my face against his chest, comforted by the muscled strength beneath my cheek, and my tremors lessened. He continued to hold me, and his words of reassurance penetrated the panicked fog in my head.

'My love' He'd called me his love?

I tilted my face upwards, hoping I was not mistaken, and with my heart seeming to hammer out of chest, wound my arms around his neck. "I long for you, Hugo. You fill my dreams…"

His mouth crashed on mine, and his kiss was everything I'd ever hoped it would be. His lips firm, his tongue urgent and demanding, intoxicated my senses. I pressed closer, moulding my body to his, exploring his mouth until we ran out of breath. I gazed into his eyes and he into mine.

"Thank the Lord I was delayed over dinner and late in arriving. How came you to be outside alone, and who was that? It's not a face I'm acquainted with."

I stroked my fingertips down his cheek. "Edgeware has been out of the country these last few years. I received a message purporting to be from the king. I am to pick up the puppies on the morrow so presumed it was in respect of that, but instead I walked into an ambush."

His embrace tightened, and though the surprise in his voice mirrored mine when Franny had first identified the viscount, his rationale was on point. "That was Edgeware? Sweeting, I smell a rat. Where is your revered uncle in all of this?"

Safe in his arms, I answered with a rueful smile. "Where he always is. Attempting to move the pieces on the board to his own advantage. Edgeware has a determination to have his own way alongside a hunger to sire a male heir, and I've proved myself capable of producing one. Uncle John has been manipulating matters in the background to achieve his aim of seizing Summerly's revenue. I put him in check by producing the king's letter. He attempted to checkmate me by way of an abduction until you arrived."

Hugo ventured. "And performed the castle manoeuvre?"

My smile widened at his comprehending my analogy. "Yes. And I thank you for it. Edgeware has tried to assert some kind of imagined authority over me afore now, but never did I expect my uncle to sink so low as to actively encourage him to do so."

He bent his head to mine. "The king's letter in place, the two of us co-joined could prove a final defence?"

My heart leapt. *A union with the man I love? A man who has always protected my son's interests?* It was the apex of my dreams. My lips a mere inch from his, I gazed up at him. "Was that a proposal, Mr FitzWilliam? Are you desirous of wedding me?"

His kiss gave me my answer. Passionate and searching, my body turned into a seething jelly of need as our tongues entwined.

He smiled into my eyes when our lips parted. "From the first time I saw you at Bedford I was envious of the man holding that honour, even as his hectoring manner towards you raised my ire. I am not a fanciful man, but I experienced such a yearning to know more of you, I confess I sought out your husband and made myself useful so I could be near you."

I traced the outline of his mouth with my fingertip. "But not so near that you would live in the same house?"

He captured my hand and kissed into the center of my palm. "Such close quarters may have surpassed my point of self-control, I fear."

"Your self-control was admirable. I never guessed."

Desire shivered through me at the intensity in his eyes.

"That will no longer be the case," he said.

I threaded my fingers through the back of his hair. His lips met mine, and I returned the demands of his mouth with all the passion I felt for him. His cock hardened against my thigh, and my knees trembled, then, breathing hard, we broke apart at the sound of the front doors of Saltash House opening.

I smoothed down the creases rumpling the front of my skirt, and Hugo rearranged the lacy ruffles adorning the neck of his shirt as a voice asked softly, "Lady Emma? Are you still outside?"

I threaded my arm through Hugo's. "I'm here, Salty. Forgive me, but Mr FitzWilliam arrived, and we became a little distracted discussing matters pertaining to the estate."

A gleam of satisfaction lit Hugo's eyes, and he placed his hand possessively over mine then led me forwards. "I add my apology to Lady Emma's. I have been remiss in detaining her."

Salty nodded, and we followed him back inside to the reception. Supper was being served, and guests sat in small groups gossiping while enjoying slices of roasted pheasant, spatchcock chicken, comfit duck eggs, and yellow butter spread on white bread, topped with quince jam. Hugo filled us a plate and led the way to a table for two. Lord Saltash joined his mother, sister, and Exeter with a slightly wistful glance in my direction. Hugo took his place, and with a raise of his eyebrow, gazed his question into my eyes.

My cheeks heated a little, and after an initial hesitation, my words came out all in a rush. "Ah… He-proposed-to-me-and-I-declined."

He dipped a piece of bread in the duck yoke and offered it to my lips. "Have you spent all your time in the capital gathering bridegrooms, my love?"

I smirked. With the teasing glint lighting his eyes, I found I couldn't help it. "Mayhap. But only one proposal was welcome."

He smiled. "Then all is well, and I will admit it. My heart fell to my boots when I heard you address Lord Francombe in such a familiar manner."

Beneath the table, I ran my fingers along his inner leg towards his groin. "Franny is the most adorable of men, but I will never be able to provide the love he seeks."

Understanding dawned in Hugo's eyes. "Like my great-great-uncle? Unacknowledged, but all who knew him well enough knew the truth of the matter."

I counted backwards to King James and nodded. "Yes, but without need to produce an heir, Franny is free to follow only his own inclination."

He nodded, and we finished our supper with heat rising through my thighs every time his leg pressed against mine.

I set my wine glass down on the table. "Have we stayed long enough? Can we make our excuses?"

He took my hand. "I believe we have been patient long enough."

I offered a slight headache as an excuse for departing early to Lady Helen and Exeter. Both of them were so lost in their own private reverie I doubted they even noticed the hour was still in advance of midnight.

A page ran ahead of us and summoned Silas to bring my coach.

Hugo put his arms around me when it set off. "We should call the banns as soon as we may, my love."

I tilted my face for his kiss and stroked his crotch. "That we will, but we will not be waiting that long to consummate the matter."

His response was immediate and urgent. His cock stiffened, and his mouth sought mine. I entwined my tongue with his and fondled his hardened shaft through his breeches. He reached for my breast and, given the neckline of my dress, it was soon nestled in his hand.

He broke our kiss and circled the nub of my nipple with his thumb. "My mouth longs for these."

I increased the pressure of my hand. "As mine does this."

Silas crying out "Whoa!" to the carriage horses recalled us.

I tucked my breast back where it should be. "When I have dismissed Hannah to seek her bed."

Hugo grasped the two sides of his suit coat and held them close together to cover his erection. "As soon as may be, if you please."

I giggled, but like the true gentleman he was, there was little sign of his excitement as he handed me from the coach.

Hannah looked a little surprised at my early return and somewhat more taken aback to see Hugo with me, so I soothed her.

"Mr FitzWilliam has news from home for me. Redress me in my informal day robe, if you would." I walked towards the dressing room and said to Hugo over my shoulder, "I shall return shortly. If you would care to pour us a glass of sherry-wine?"

He moved to do so, and I asked Hannah when she closed the dressing room door behind us, "The sponge and the remainder of lemon juice. Do you still have them?"

She nodded. "I was not sure whether you would attend another royal supper, so I decanted the lemon into a stoppered vial."

I smiled my relief. "Mr FitzWilliam is desirous of marrying me, and I him. There will be lemon juice and sponge required each day until my next monthly course begins. I wish to leave no room for doubt that any child I conceive was sired by him."

Hannah voiced her concern. "He is a fine gentleman, but my lady...you would lose your title?"

Her status as a servant dependent on mine, so I sought to reassure her. "I will but I was born noble, and no circumstance can change that, nor more can it alter the fact I am a mother of an earl. Mr FitzWilliam himself is royally connected. I believe there will no loss of respect."

Hannah bobbed then hastened to remove my clothes, and afterwards I used my personal closet. I gave her leave to take her night's rest with a request not to bring food and drink to break my fast until she received a call to do so.

I stepped into my sitting room. Hugo had removed his suit coat along with the ruffled fall of lace that had decorated the neck of his shirt. Sitting on the two-person sofa, he offered me a fluted glass, and my eyes were drawn to the broad shoulders and muscled upper arms outlined beneath the near-translucent fine linen. The special place between my legs throbbed.

I walked closer, stood before him, accepted the glass, and tugged on the belt of my robe. It parted when I threw back my head and swallowed the contents down.

His voice rasped in the back of his throat. "Oh, sweet Jesu… Emma…"

He buried his face in my muff, and the glass fell from my fingers onto the carpeted floor as his warm tongue explored the soft folds and creases of the nub of my desire. I knotted my fingers through the back of his hair, my knees threatening to give way, and voiced my deepest longing.

"Let me see you naked? Give me your love skin to skin with nothing concealed?"

With an inarticulate cry, he stood and scooped me into his arms as if I weighed no more than a feather. He carried me into the bedroom candlelit bedroom and laid me down. I dispensed with my robe and reclined on the pillows. He stood to the side of the bed, unfasted the ribbons at the neck of his shirt, and pulled it over his head.

My heart rate increased. I didn't know where to look first. His taut belly, broad shoulders, or hard chest covered with soft, downy hair I longed to feel brush over my skin. He toed off his shoes, eased down his breeches, and removed them along with his silk knee-length stockings. He walked towards me, his cock resplendent, thick and hard, and I parted my legs with a whimper.

"Hugo…please…"

He lay over me and gazed into my eyes. "You want me, sweeting?"

Desperate to feel him inside me, I wrapped my legs around his thighs and dug my fingertips into his shoulders. "Don't tease me. Not this time. I want you so much."

He plunged into me up to his hilt. "And I you."

I mewled my relief and lifted my hips. He thrust harder, meeting my urgent demands, and the throb between my legs built. My soft breasts and sensitised nipples brushing against the curls of hair on his chest thrilled me, and I cried out his name as waves of pleasure pulsed through my groin.

"Hugo… Hugo…"

He thrust again. "Emma…my adored love…"

I whimpered and panted the last moments of my climax. Hugo kissed my lips, then my neck, and we stilled. He withdrew and lay beside me. I nestled under his arm and ran my fingers through the hair on his chest then brushed my lips over it.

"It holds a fascination for you, love?"

I smiled and moved my fingers to explore the contours of his shoulders. "Yes. I find it delightful along with all the other contrasts between us. I did not know them. I have never seen a man completely disrobed before."

"Not even…?"

I closed that particular avenue of speculation down with a firm, "No. Never."

He kissed into the top of my hair. "You will be seeing more of this one."

I put my leg across his thighs with a happy sigh when the hair on his legs tickled the smoothness of mine. "Yes...please."

He reached out, tucked the coverlet around us and, secure in his arms, I let my eyelids flutter closed.

I woke in the morning with my head resting on his chest, soft hairs tickling my cheek, and nuzzled my lips into them, delighting in our nakedness. His nether regions stirred before he did. I giggled and stroked his shaft awake. With a soft growl, he reversed our positions and lay over me.

"Is there some service you are desirous of me performing for you, my lady?"

The apex between my legs pulsed with anticipation. I parted them and eased his cockhead through my wetness. "Indeed, there is."

His shaft pushed deeper, and I sighed. "Hugo...yes..."

He slid his thick length back and forth, slow and languorous. "You like, sweeting?"

I wrapped my legs around his thighs. "So very much."

"And this?" He bent his head and sucked my nipple into his mouth.

I writhed beneath him. "More…please…"

He plunged deeper, tugging on my nipple with his teeth until I dug my fingers into his back and begged, "Oh, Jesu…take me now, Hugo."

With a murmur of satisfaction, he thrust faster and faster, and I moaned as muscles outside my control tightened and throbbed. "Hugo…yes, yes yes…"

Hugo slammed his cock into me with more urgency, and pleasure spread through my belly to his groaned, "My sweet love…"

He rolled to his side, and once my breathing steadied, I turned onto mine facing him and stroked his cheek.

"When I have the puppies, I would like to collect George and Bonnie from Hatfield and return home?"

He kissed the tip of my nose. "I must visit the warehouse and set in place the scheme by which I intend to take delivery of the sugar. If I accomplish the task whilst you are at the kennels, we could leave for Hatfield on the morrow if such a sudden departure would not discomfort your hosts?"

I smiled. "My godmother has been at loggerheads with Uncle John for years. She'll perfectly understand my concerns, as will Franny. I'll instruct Hannah to commence packing so as to be able to depart the capital on the morrow."

"Then much as I wish I did not to have to quit this bed, I should return to Westminster so I may send Tom to you with the boxes of confection destined for the king, the duchess, and Lady Castlemaine before I attend the docks."

The doorknob rattled, and he asked, "Hannah?"

Having requested her not to return until summoned, I knew exactly who was about to enter my bedroom and called out to stall him. "Ah… I'm naked, my Adonis."

Franny's muffled voice sounded through the woodwork, and I buried my face in the pillow to stifle my laughter as he stuttered, "Yes…well…I'll just bide my time out here then."

I peeked up at Hugo. He grinned when the sofa springs squeaked and we heard Franny's voice.

"My angel, you seem to have obtained some items of male attire that appear to be a little too large for your frame?"

I giggled, reached for my robe, and admitted the truth of the matter. "Mr FitzWilliam is with me." I blew Hugo a kiss, threaded my arms through its sleeves and tightened the belt, then walked out of my bedroom to join Franny, leaving Hugo to re-dress.

Franny's mouth framed the silent words after I closed the door behind me. *Your Mr Fitz?*

I knew my face was aglow with happiness. I didn't need a mirror to see it. I could feel it. *Yes. Mine.* I nodded.

He smiled, and Hugo stepped into the sitting room. Franny greeted him.

"Mr FitzWilliam, I give you a good morn."

Hugo, with the assurance of a man with no need of title to command respect, picked up his suit jacket and bowed his respects. "As I do you, my lord." Then, took my hand to his lips, and kissed each of my fingers. "Tom will be with you shortly. You will ensure Silas drives you to the kennels and instruct him if any person, be they ever so high a lord, attempts to dismiss him, he is not to obey?"

I stroked my fingertips down his cheek. "Be assured of it. I will not be taken in by such a trick again."

He released my hand. "I will return here when our business is accomplished."

I smiled into his eyes. "As soon as may be, if you please."

"You may depend on it."

I watched him leave the room, transfixed, until Franny issued a polite cough.

"So…?"

I spun towards him. "He saved me, Franny. After you left the reception at Saltash House, I received a message purporting to be from the king. I stepped outside and was nearly captured, but Hugo, late in arriving, intervened."

The usual sparkle fled from Franny's eyes, and his irises darkened. "Captured? By whom?"

With all my heart I did not wish him to feel obliged to confront an ex-beau on my behalf when Hugo had already dealt with the matter, so I poured us each a glass sherry-wine, sat on the sofa, and offered one to him. "Come, sit. Let us talk in comfort as we always do."

He accepted my offer and sat.

I sipped then squeezed his hand. "I think mayhap you've guessed, it was Edgeware, but I beg you to listen to me when I tell you it was my Uncle John who was the master puppeteer pulling the strings in the background. He played on Edgeware's weaknesses and vanity. Hugo has

233

left Edgeware in no doubt of what will happen to him should he cause me any further discomfort."

Franny spluttered. "Knowing the contents of your letter, the duke ignored the express wishes of the king?"

I shrugged. "He could deny ever having read it."

He swallowed the contents of his glass. "Then His Majesty should know of the matter. Indeed, it is of importance that he does. The Monarchy, so newly restored, must not be undermined by the duke disregarding the king's edict. I will seek a private word at the next opportunity."

I gave him a small smile. "No, my Adonis. It concerns me most nearly, and I will be in his company today. I will risk Lady Castlemaine's displeasure one more time and draw him away to converse privately with me."

He nodded. "He will thank you for it, I believe, as should Barbara if her mind was less greedy as to allow her to understand the consequences."

"She will look down her nose at me for preferring the affection of an illegitimate cousin, three times removed, I'm sure. But I care nothing for that. Hugo will make his mark on this world, and I would rather be with a man who desires only me."

Franny smirked. "As would I."

I laughed and set down my glass. "You wretch! Off with you! If you please, ask the page to send Hannah to me?"

He grinned and did so.

Chapter Eleven

Hannah was not long delayed in attending me, bringing with her my cocoa and rolls. I ate while she prepared my toilette and, as promised, Tom arrived with the boxes of nou-gaar. He was followed not much later by a pageboy wearing royal purple while she pinned and tied the ribbons to fasten my gold brocade dress.

"His Royal Majesty requests your presence at eleven, my lady."

I dismissed the lad with a message expressing my honour and delight to do so along with a silver sixpence for his trouble. Hannah then completed the final touches to my appearance while I sat and contemplated how best to obtain a few minutes of private conversation with the king without raising his mistress' ire. It occurred to me that she may distain to risk soiling her gown by kneeling on a floor which may be concealing a dog turd or several within the straw strewn thickly all over its surface. If I arrived ahead of time and was found on my knees playing with the puppies, I thought the odds were in my favour of the king joining me as he had before, while she would not. So, I ordered my coach be made ready immediately, and well in advance of the appointed hour had Silas drive me to Whitehall, taking with me a pageboy to carry the boxes of confectionary and a lidded wicker basket.

The scent of lactating dogs greeted my nostrils as I alighted the vehicle, and I requested one of the kennel lads to bring Will the younger to me. He arrived and made his bow.

"We 'ad word you would be 'ere this day, my lady. Thy pups are ready for thee."

I nodded. "His Majesty will attend shortly to present them to me. Lead the way to them, if you please."

I signalled the pageboy to stay with the coach, and Will led the way inside. My two beribboned pups had been isolated from the rest by way of wooden boarding to form a stable-like enclosure. The space was thankfully generous. Well enough to accommodate two adults, and moreover, I thought it would add an element of privacy for my intended conversation with the king, if, as I hoped, he stepped inside.

Will lifted the front board away for me to enter. "'Tis ter grow 'em used to being away from tha rest an' be on their own."

My new pets had become even more gorgeous since I had last seen them. Plumper, their markings prettier, they romped in the straw chasing each other's tails with small high-pitched yips. I smiled at the sight, stepped closer, and toed through the straw looking for stinky nuggets. A goodly area at the back proved clear of both them and any yellow stain of piss. It seemed my new pets had a penchant for doing their necessary business to one side of the stall which boded well for when I took them home. King Charles might allow his pets to soil whether ever they would, but that would not be happening at Summerly.

A commotion sounded outside to herald the arrival of the royal party, so I dropped to my knees and sat back on my heels. The puppies tumbled towards me to investigate, and I giggled when the female climbed onto my lap and nibbled my fingertips, then the male pounced on her for being daft enough to stay still and allow him to do so. At the sound of footsteps scrunching on straw, I looked up and into the eyes of the king. He swept off his wide-brimmed hat, passed it to Lord Buckingham, and joined me.

I picked up the male and held him to me. "They are more adorable than ever. I thank you for letting me have them, Your Majesty."

He crouched to my side and tickled behind the ear of the female who closed her eyes in a moment of doggy bliss. "They are a pretty pair."

As I hoped, Barbara stayed where she was, and I thought her expression seemed one part aghast at the treatment being meted out to the expensive fabric of my gown, and two parts hopeful that brown sludge would be decorating the front of it when I stood. I kissed my pup on his sweet little nose and smiled into the eyes of the king as I confirmed his advice on the raising of them.

"Their meat should be minced fine with an equal measure of crumbled oat biscuit, and they are to be fed twice daily?"

He looked pleased at my remembering. "With the addition of a cup of goat milk apiece, but that only for the next two sennight."

I glanced out of the corner of my eye and noted that Barbara had lost interest in the mundane nature of our conversation and had turned to the king's escorting pack in search of a subject more entertaining, namely herself. Sir Charles Berkley was obliging in creating a short ode in praise of the perfection of her 'cherry-red' lips and was currently seeking a word to rhyme with luscious.

I lowered my voice. "I find I have an urgent need to return home to my son, Sire."

"How so?"

"Two days ago, the Duke of Portchester attempted to snatch control of Summerly from me, then further chose to disregard the contents of your letter when shown it. Last evening, he arranged an abduction to hold me in close confinement until such time as I agreed to his demands."

The king's eyes darkened with displeasure. "He did what?"

Ribald laughter from outside the stall caught his attention. "Take yourselves off and find your distraction elsewhere."

The unusually sharp tone of his voice brooked no discussion on the matter, and the group, including Barbara, moved away.

"Explain more, if you please."

Hugo might not wish to soil his lips by mentioning Edgeware's vile conduct, but I held no such scruples. "He played on another's weakness to accomplish the deed in place of himself. Not so many minutes after you departed Saltash House, I was lured outside by way of a message supposedly from yourself."

"And you obeyed without question?"

I gazed into his eyes. "Of course. Always. Without hesitation."

The king's expression softened at my assurance, which in all essence was the truth, barring I would find good reason to excuse myself should he wish to bed me again.

"The Duke of Wight requires his son to marry and produce an heir. Having done so once, my uncle convinced Viscount Edgeware of a successful outcome should he wed me. Such is Edgeware's vanity, he would not take no for answer when I refused the match. He waited in the shadows for me to obey your summons then tried to manhandle me into his coach, but Mr FitzWilliam, late in arriving, stepped forward and prevented him from doing so. I do not believe Edgeware will make a second attempt, but I do not trust the Duke of Portchester. Every maternal feeling is urging me to return home without delay and put additional measures in place to ensure George and Summerly remain in my care."

His searching gaze examined my face for what seemed an eternity before he finally nodded and spoke. "That you will not rest easy till you have seen your son is understandable, but you will not depart the capital before attending my next levee."

From the steely glint in his eye, it was not a far stretch to guess he was going to make public censure of my uncle's insubordination which would soon wing its way to his ears.

My heart sang. "As ever 'twill be my honour to attend you there, Sire."

He smiled and pinched my chin. "I believe I will miss your person probably more than I should when you leave us."

Uninvited to do so, I was taking a liberty, I knew, but I leaned close, brushed my lips across his, and whispered cheekily into his ear, "With so much sweet fruit as yet untasted by your boy, I do not fear it."

He chuckled, and the sound of it drew Barbara's attention. Her head turned towards the stall, and what must have appeared to her to be a flirtatious tête-à-tête.

Her sharp comment was made to Lord Berkley but directed at us. "This becomes tiresome. If kept waiting for much longer, I believe I will depart for Richmond in search of a diversion more to my taste."

I asked the king, "I have a basket for the puppies and also a gift in my coach. With your leave, I will call for them?"

He nodded, stood, offered me his hand to rise, then escorted me from the stall.

I saw Will and beckoned him. "Call my page to bring the basket and painted boxes to me, if you would."

He bowed, trotted off, and soon returned carrying the wicker basket which he took into the stall. The Melville page, one step behind him, held the rose-decorated caskets. He paused before me. I lifted one and offered it to Barbara. That she loved to receive presents was well-known, and a gift she was not expecting ensured her good humour — so long as she approved of it.

She took it from me. "How pretty. What have you bought me, I wonder? A lace collar or mayhap gloves?"

She lifted the lid and peered at the contents.

I smiled. "'Tis the latest sensation from France."

King Charles glanced over her shoulder. "So it is. Minette wrote to me of the French Court's current obsession to consume pink-and-white nou-gaar. Given their appetite for the confection, I had not heard it was available outside of that country."

That the king's most beloved sister had made mention of it, I thought piqued Barbara's interest, for she had been looking less than impressed. She roused herself to nibble on a square, and her reaction was the one I was hoping for. Her eyes widened, and she popped the rest of the portion into her mouth.

I took the chance to offer the second casket to the king. "Mayhap the queen?"

He took it. "I behold the results of Mr FitzWilliam's enterprise?"

"Sugar is the majority ingredient, Sire."

"And you now possess such a quantity of it."

"Extraordinarily we do."

A smile lurking at the corners of his lips, the king answered, "Require Mr FitzWilliam to escort you to my levee at the Banqueting House."

I took a step backwards so as not to further exhaust Barbara's patience with the attention I was receiving. Will took his chance to present me with the wicker basket. I anticipated high-pitched puppy whines but instead was greeted with sleepy snuffles and a soft snore.

I beckoned the Melville page forward. "Take my pups to Silas Coachman, if you please."

I curtsied my thanks and farewell to my Sovereign then departed the kennels, and as I was driven away it occurred to me, I had not enquired from Lady Castlemaine the names she had chosen for the pups. I shrugged. Her choice would have been discarded anyway. I had always intended for Bonnie and George to name their own pets.

I had the pageboy carry the basket upstairs when I arrived at the Melville residence.

I opened the lid, and Hannah dropped to her knees.

"Oh, my lady. The dear of them." She scooped them up, her face a picture of a woman in love, and cooed. "Are you hungry, poppets? Shall Hannah find thee a little something?"

I surveyed my godmother's expensive floor coverings. "The king does not train his pets into sociable habits. Will you have a care for them until our return to Summerly?"

Her voice was nothing but delighted. "I shall. The footman can fill a dirt box, and I will begin their education on the requirement to use it. It will not take long."

I gave her the king's instructions for their feeding, and she took them to the servant's hall then returned with bread, cheese, and fruit for me. Once refreshed, I sought out my godmother and explained my need to return home.

Her face became more and more furious as I relayed the events of the last two days until she heard King Charles had requested my attendance at his levee and declared, "A show of strength is needed. I will accompany you, as will Franny and those who are our particular friends."

Her ferocious support warmed me, and I thanked her, which, as usual, she waved away.

"'Twill be nothing but my pleasure to thumb my nose at your uncle, Emma. I've loathed him and his sanctimonious money-grubbing ways for years."

I smiled and kissed her cheek. "And for that I thank you even more."

She laughed, and I left her.

Neither Hannah nor the pups were in evidence on my return to my suite, so I sat behind the desk to enjoy the peaceful interlude while penning a few lines to Bonnie of my intention to join her and George by late afternoon on the morrow. My missive dispatched by a fast horse and rider, I sat on the sofa and closed my eyes for a few moments to gather my thoughts. Strong arms lifting me brought me to, but I knew the feel of them now and rested my head on Hugo's shoulder.

"You are worn out, my love, and no wonder with all that has occurred these last two days."

I peeked up at him as he carried me to the bedroom. "Not so very much if you are here."

He laid me on the bed. I pulled his head towards mine, and his kiss, deep and searching, left my chest heaving... I watched him strip the layers of clothing hiding what I longed to see, and my skin heated with desire at the sight of him naked, his prick ramrod straight. I licked my lips, beckoned him closer, and wrapped my mouth around his cock head. His soft murmur of pleasure rippled through my belly and into my groin. I grasped his shaft and increased the pressure of my mouth, while mimicking the slow back-and-forth rhythm of our morn love-making with my hand until he groaned.

"Sweet Jesu, Emma…"

I released him and, nothing loathe to extend the moment of our final pleasure, teased, "You may flip my skirts above my head and take me or help me remove this gown. I cannot do so. It fastens behind."

He lay over me, twitched the bodice of it downwards, and exposed the round globes of my breasts. "A gentleman does not take his pleasure before his lady has achieved her own."

My nipples responded, hardening into stiffened peaks. He lowered his head, sucked, then tugged with his teeth, moving from breast to breast, till I thrashed beneath him and squealed.

"Hugo…"

His fingers sought the ribbons at the back of my gown, and when they resisted for being secured with the addition of pins, he ripped them from their moorings. My dress, shift, and petticoats were soon around my thighs, then thrown to the floor. He plunged his cock into my welcoming wetness, and I bucked against him with an urgency to match his own.

He growled, soft and low. "Wrap your legs around me."

I did so, and my hips lifted, allowing him to thrust deeper and harder. I mewled my appreciation and rocked my pelvis. The nub hidden in the folds of my muff throbbed, the sensation building, and whether I willed it or no, words poured from my mouth to the climax spreading through my groin and belly. "Hugo. Yes…yes…yes… Oh, oh…"

He tensed, then groaned. "My sweet love…"

Panting, I clung on tight.

He kissed my shoulder, my neck, then my lips.

I gazed into his eyes. "I love you."

The green of his irises warmed—a look I was coming to know was reserved for me and only me.

"And I you."

With a contented sigh, I straightened my legs and let him go, then rested my cheek on his chest. "I believe I could sleep for a while now."

He held me closer and kissed into my hair. "No one shall harm you while I am close by. I promise it."

I sighed again, and my eyelids fluttered closed.

The bedroom was still full of daylight when I stirred. I yawned, saw Hugo's soft smile, and asked, "What hour is it?"

He stroked down my back. "'Tis not yet five, my love. Hannah came a-looking, but I shushed her, and she crept away."

I rubbed my cheek against his chest, caressed his shoulders, and trailed my fingertips down his arms. There was something about his bodily hair being in places where it was absent from mine I found masculine and totally entrancing.

He cuddled me tighter. "How went your meeting with the king?"

I relayed the detail and finished with, "He wishes both of us to attend his levee in the morn. I believe he will make public comment to put my uncle in his place. My godmother agrees and is so delighted, she is calling in every favour owed. On the morrow, the Court will be filled with supporters that wish us well."

Hugo whistled through pursed lips. "That will be some occasion to behold. When I tell m'father of it he will wish to attend."

I smiled. "I believe my own appearance should be sumptuous enough to defy Uncle John's every edict on feminine modesty. What think you? A silver gown with every sparkling diamond my mother managed to hide and keep out of his grasp or the amber beaded gold accompanied by the jewels of colour I inherited from my grandmother?"

He tilted my chin and kissed my lips. "I have not viewed you in silver, though I have heard tell of it."

I smirked my delight and kissed him back. "You have?"

"As soon as I arrived in Town. The Countess of Summerly. A glittering angel whose beauty surpasses man's ability to praise. I thought then you were beyond my dreams."

I threaded my fingers through the back of his hair and urged his face closer for a deeper kiss. "Never that. I wanted to know your love at Summerly and longed for you even more when I arrived here and we were parted. No man compares to you or ever will."

His tongue sought mine and mine his, and he smiled into my eyes when our mouths parted.

"We must live at Summerly until George requires it for his own use when he marries or reaches his majority, but while we do, the hunting lodge could be demolished for a house of our own design to be erected?"

The thought thrilled me. Hugo and I would have children, I was sure. That Hugo's hard work and enterprise would make us wealthy, of that, I was equally sure. George was young enough to not stand alone from his half-siblings. They would be brought up together at Summerly with the reassurance for the younger ones their futures did not depend on one brother above any other. "I would like that *so very much*."

He smiled. "I hoped you might."

Our interlude was bought to an end by a tap on the door. "My angel, are you decent?"

I giggled and answered, "No, my Adonis, I am not. Once again, I am naked and Mr FitzWilliam with me."

Hugo swatted my buttock as Franny huffed through the woodwork. "I declare you are spending more time disrobed than myself. Outrageous, my sweet!"

I laughed, swung my legs off the bed, and reached for my shift, then, with my flesh covered, sauntered out of the bedroom, leaving Hugo to re-dress.

Franny had filled three glasses with ruby-red wine and offered me one. "Mama relayed all excepting how the confection was received."

I accepted the glass and sipped. "Lady Castlemaine was initially doubtful until His Majesty mentioned Minette had written to him of its success in France. The queen will be the recipient of the second box, I believe."

Franny nodded. "The production of an heir can be a cold business far removed from the act of love, as you know, but King Charles is not unkind. Queen Catherine may be estranged from Court, but he will not be plunging his mighty sceptre in and out of her each night without any sympathy for her situation."

My laugh snorted down my nose. "Franny!"

The bedroom door opened, and perfectly dressed, Hugo joined us. I could tell from the twitch of his lips he had overheard and enjoyed every word.

He bowed to Franny. "My lord." And joined in with his own double entendre. "Barbara Palmer will gobble it all down in an instant. The queen, with a suitable sigh, will consume it piece by piece."

I giggled, and Franny laughed.

"Well summed up, sir, though the picture it conjures is not one I care to bring to mind."

Hannah walked into the room carrying my pitcher of washing water.

Franny excused himself. "I will see you at seven, my sweet. And you, sir? Will you join the company here tonight?"

Hugo bowed. "I thank you. I will."

Franny kissed the back of my hand and Hugo my lips, then they left. Hannah eyed my linen shift.

I offered my apology. "My dress will need some attention from your needle, I fear."

She tutted, though from the twinkle in her eye, I knew she didn't mean it.

"I will make the attempt, but first, my lady, your toilette while the water is still hot?"

I nodded, walked into the dressing room, and while she cleansed me, gave her my requirements for the following day. "By His Majesty's invitation, I attend his levee on the morrow. To give due respect, I will wear the gown of my Presentation along with every diamond I possess."

The timbre of her voice raised a little from her normal tone. "All of them?"

I smiled, my happiness completed by the knowledge that in less than one day, my child would be in my arms. "Every. Single. One. 'Tis a day for ostentation. Apart from my silver ensemble, lay out my mulberry travelling gown and pack the rest of my belongings. We will travel to Hatfield and collect George and Bonnie after the levee."

Hannah bobbed. "I will have your trunks bought to the room and begin the task while you are at thy dinner, my lady."

I contemplated the evening ahead when dressed and found I had little appetite for the games of cards compared to the idea of enticing Hugo to my suite once dinner was complete. Still, I picked up the caskets of nou-gaar, one for the duchess and one to be passed around the card tables, and dismissed the notion. If I was to set out for Hatfield after the levee, Hannah must be accorded the time to bustle about in my rooms and accomplish her work.

I descended the stairs, entered the Tapestry room, and after my name was announced, made my way to my godmother and presented her with my parting gift.

She looked delighted. "Franny told me of this, the new confection. I thank you. The casket alone would prove a delightful adornment to any lady's sitting room."

She beckoned a pageboy and instructed him to place it on the occasional table beside her chaise lounge.

I handed him the incomplete portion. "To be offered to the ladies once dinner is finished."

He trotted off, and Hugo's name was announced. I gazed at him, and his eyes searched the room until he found mine. My heart swelled as he came closer , to my mind, the most handsome man in the room, the capital, or indeed, any other place in the kingdom. From the faint ripple of female appreciation, I was not the only woman to think so. His suit jacket of dark blue stretched tight across his broad shoulders, his white breeches were immaculate, and it gave me a secret thrill that I knew what lay beneath the taut material.

I tried not to look too besotted when he reached me and kissed the back of my hand, though I was not sure I'd managed it when Franny glanced in my direction and grinned. I pulled myself together, took his offered arm, and walked to where Exeter, Saltash, and Lady Helen were engaged in low-voiced conversation.

"The duchess enquired whether we were attending the king's levee on the morrow."

"She enquired the same of myself."

"Strange. She attended to present Lady Emma, but it is not usually an occasion that attracts her attention."

That I believed King Charles meant to issue a rebuke to my uncle was not assured, so I smiled and admitted only the fact I was sure of, plus a point I thought was not far from the mark. "His Majesty has requested myself and Mr FitzWilliam to attend. Like us, she wishes to know why, but as Summerly has just purchased a large quantity of the queen's dowry, I suspect it is in acknowledgement of that."

Franny came up to us in time to hear my words and grinned but did not add any of our private speculation. "How exciting. Let us all gather here and partake of refreshments in the morn. Then we can arrive at Whitehall together."

The plan was soon agreed, and at dinner my godmother sat Hugo to my left with Lady Helen to his other side.

I turned to him. "Hannah is packing my possessions."

"Cuthbert is performing the same service for myself."

Lady Helen expressed her surprise. "You are leaving Town?"

I nodded. "My son has need of us. After the levee, we must go home. There are arrangements for his well-being to be put in place."

"I will miss your company."

I smiled. "And I yours, but I will visit London again when I'm able to, and you are always welcome at Summerly."

Her cheeks flushed pink. "Yes. When I am Lady Exeter, I will be able to come and go as I please."

Exeter caught her eye and winked, making her words a cheeky double entendre, and she giggled. The rest of us laughed, and her cheeks turned pink.

Dinner complete, we retired to play cards. The nou-gaar was a success and received a great deal of attention, not just from the ladies who took a taste but from the men who saw their reaction and sought to purchase it for their wives and lovers and mother and sisters. I excused myself around one in the morn, leaving Hugo to follow me up to my rooms a few minutes afterwards, and saw my trunks stacked neatly barring one that still stood open awaiting the clothes I was wearing and the silver ensemble after the levee.

I thanked Hannah for her hard work and exchanged my gown for my day robe, saving its possible ruination by Hugo's rather masculine method of assisting me out of it, then dismissed her to find her own rest. Hugo stepped into my rooms as she left them. I held out my hand and led him to the bed.

I dropped my robe to the floor and watched him strip, my anticipation building when his nakedness appeared. He lay beside me, kissed me long and deep, and we made love at a slower pace than previously, taking our time, exploring each other's bodies with soft caresses, lips, and tongues. He mounted me at the peak of my desire, and I writhed beneath him, burrowing my face into his neck to stifle my moans.

He thrust faster. "Do not hold back, sweeting. Let me know your pleasure."

Waves of extasy spread through my groin, and I sank my teeth into his shoulder.

He tensed. "Yes… Emma… Yes…"

I bit down harder and sucked.

He groaned, deep and low. "Oh, Jesu…yes…"

I kissed the love bruise I'd left when we stilled. "Have I hurt you?"

He kissed my neck. "I like to feel your desire. Your teeth on me, your fingers digging into my back."

I kissed the spot again. "'Tis as well as I did not bite your neck. At least this will be covered by your shirt on the morrow."

He smiled and withdrew his softened shaft. "I would not care."

I sighed with contentment and snuggled under his arm, and we slept until dawn lightened the window.

Hugo stirred. "With the levee being at midday, I'd best not delay Hannah ministering to you by my presence."

He swung his legs off the bed, dressed, and I fell back to sleep until she brought my early-morn meal to me. I smiled as I ate—such a short time ago I had been so excited to be here in my godmother's house, and now I was equally excited about going home. Despite the trouble my uncle and Edgeware had caused, I had enjoyed the entertainments and parties of my stay, and the friendship I had encountered warmed me. I would return before too long, rent a house, and bring Bonnie and George with me, but in the meantime, I was thrilled to be returning to Summerly to marry the man of my dreams.

My hunger satisfied, I walked to my dressing room and, an hour later, cleansed and dressed once again in the silver gown of my Presentation, this time I allowed Hannah to place the diamond collar around my neck. Several diamond rings adorned my fingers along with the encrusted bangles around my wrists, but I did not select the tiara—it was not the occasion for it. Instead, she dressed my hair in a more intricate pattern, held in place with a dozen diamond clips.

I turned back and forth in front of the mirror and was pleased with my reflection. Silver and diamonds, rather than gold, were certainly the better choice to stand out in the midst of a colourful crowd should the king be looking for me. My nerves jangled at the uncertainty of what would occur at the levee but also in hope that my uncle's high-handed interference in my life, George's, and Bonnie's would at last be at an end.

I picked up my fan with a quick smile at Hannah and descended the stairs to the Tapestry room. Its door stood open, and my nerves settled when I saw Hugo. I hurried towards his reassuring presence, secure in the knowledge that whatever else occurred I was no longer alone.

His father, standing alongside him, bowed over my hand. "It is a great pleasure to meet you again, my lady. My son has made certain matters clear. It will be my honour to know you better in due course."

I smiled. "As it will be mine to know you."

Lady Helen sported a new gown of cherry red in the latest style. I admired it, and she confided Lord Exeter had stood the expense of it and three more beside as a betrothal gift. A party atmosphere pervaded, and after two glasses of sherry-wine accompanied by half an hour of light-hearted banter, I felt calm and serene. My godmother, resplendent in a heavily brocaded satin gown of leaf green, set down her glass when the mantel clock struck eleven.

Franny winked at me. "The final act of the play approaches, my sweet."

His mama took his arm. He led her outside followed by Rochester who escorted the duchess' nearest friend, Viscountess Deignby, and the rest of us sauntered along behind.

Three carriages were lined up outside the Melville residence. Hugo handed me into the second of them, and we set off for Whitehall. The colonnaded hall of the Banqueting House was alive with noise when we entered it, and I was somewhat taken aback to spot my uncle in attendance, although he looked more alarmed to see me. He glanced at the door, then he scurried towards it, but the pikemen stood one to either side of it and crossed their weapons, barring his exit—a guest, once inside, was not permitted to leave, it seemed.

Franny watched the byplay, leaned close, and murmured, "So, the pieces on the board are assembled. The end-game is nigh."

Black Rod banged his staff upon the floor which was in itself unusual, given the king's normal preference for informality. The door behind the throne swung open, and he strode through it, no pets frolicking at his heels, all sign of geniality absent from his expression.

"Od's blood. He means business," Rochester noted.

Franny's lips curled into satisfied smile. "Our Sovereign favours the role of Merry Monarch, but he also possesses the iron-willed ruthlessness of a true king, and any man foolish enough to mistake the matter does so at his own peril."

My godmother added, "You do not lead the charge into battle at the head of your father's army at fourteen without such qualities, nor hunt down the regicides who murdered him and exact your revenge by the grisliest method possible."

King Charles did not move to sit on his throne but raked his gaze around the room until it rested on me. He beckoned, and the room fell silent as if holding its collective breath. The crowd parted as I walked towards him and made my Court curtsy. He raised me and brushed my lips with his as he had before, and I knew for whom the point was being made.

He offered me his arm. "We will take a turn around the room."

I laid my hand on his forearm, and we began an evenly paced circuit of the hall, the crowd bowing or dipping until we reached my uncle.

The king paused, looked into my eyes, and sniffed. "I do believe I detect the stench of treason in the air." Then he turned his head towards Uncle John, who, as if sensing his danger, blustered, "Sire, I beseech you. As I have ever been. I am your most loyal, most humble, most devoted subject."

Unmoved, the king continued to contemplate the duke's face, until he twitched, nervously uncomfortable—and only then did he issue his Royal Decree. "Restitution will be made in the form of one hundred thousand crowns. You have two sennight to gather it."

My uncle's face blanched at the size of the fine, and the king administered a final admonishment.

"My eye is on you, Portchester. Disappoint me again, and you will feel the full weight of my displeasure. Your accommodation in the Tower would not be of the finest, nor your stay as my guest of any great duration."

King Charles led me on and next paused in front of Hugo. He offered out his ring hand. Hugo bowed low and brushed his lips across the Coronation jewel.

"Sire. You do me much honour."

In regal tones, the king made his closing point. "True friends and supporters will always find it so. Winchelsea is currently extant, I find. You will receive my letter patent."

The newly created Baron of Winchelsea glanced at me, a gleam of surprised pleasure in his eyes, and I smiled my delight back at him. If anything in our shared look had alerted him, I couldn't tell, but the king gave us a small nod.

"Nothing about a union made between you would offend. You have my consent should you wish to make it."

No words were required. Hugo and I were but bit players on the side of his royal stage. I curtsied my thanks. Hugo bowed his. The king turned away and left the Banqueting House the way he had arrived, without a word or glancing at any other.

The room let out its collective breath when it closed behind him, and a hum of conversation restarted. Franny looked delighted and my godmother triumphant. She stared at my uncle and made a very rude gesture behind her fan— the same one the English longbowmen showed to their enemies in battle.

Franny snorted. "Mama!"

She was totally unrepentant. "How long I have prayed for that man to get his well-deserved comeuppance. The lives he has ruined to satisfy his own ambition. His disgrace is of his own making, and I will feel no sorrow for his plight."

To the side of me, Baron FitzWilliam's face was wreathed in smiles, as well it might. Hugo's brother might have a wait to inherit, but he now had two sons of equal standing. Wine was called for as Saltash, Exeter, and Rochester crowded around to offer their congratulations.

Franny looked into my eyes. "And so it ends and we win the game, my angel. We had fun along the way, though, did we not?"

I thought he sounded a little wistful and kissed his cheek. "We certainly did, my Adonis."

Salty drifted across my eyeline, then Bonnie into my mind. Mayhap? I shook the thought away. She would have free rein over the subject of her marriage, but it was not very likely a dowerless girl would have the same choice of suitors as one better endowed. Unless…

I smiled. "But never fear, my lord. I will be back to plague you soon. I foresee the need for the creation of a new dance. The steps designed with flair to fascinate and dazzle."

His sparkle returned along with his grin. "They will be exquisite, dearest heart. Once more we shall set the Town alight. You have my promise."

Printed in Great Britain
by Amazon